THREE WICKED BEARS

A DARK FAIRYTALE RETELLING

CASSIA BRIAR

Wednesday Ink

THREE WICKED BEARS

CONTENTS

Content Information   ix

1. Gem   1
2. Gem   11
3. Kevin   17
4. Gem   23
5. Gem   33
6. Blake   41
7. Gem   55
8. Gem   67
9. Gem   77
10. Nathaniel   87
11. Gem   95
12. Kevin   109
13. Gem   115
14. Gem   127
15. Blake   137
16. Gem   145
17. Gem   151
18. Gem   161
19. Nathaniel   171
20. Gem   183
21. Gem   195
22. Kevin   201
23. Gem   207
24. Blake   213
25. Gem   219
26. Nathaniel   229
27. Gem   237

About the Author 245
Suggested Reading Order 247

CONTENT INFORMATION

If you don't like TWs then please skip this page!

This book contains, but is not limited to, captivity, dubious consent, violence, gang rape, post rape trauma, cutting, BDSM, spanking, physical and verbal abuse, mutilation, cigar burns, scars, genital removal, torture, abduction, psychological abuse, self-esteem issues, past trauma, PTSD, bullying, survival, kinks, swearing, possessiveness, fear, pimping, shaming, and humiliation.

1

GEM

"You worthless little bitch," Arik snarled. He reached across to where I sat in the passenger seat and squeezed my thigh. Using his wolf shifter strength, it was hard enough to leave a bruise on my pale skin. "You were supposed to please him. And did you? Did you please him, Gem?"

His fingers dug further into my skin. I gritted my teeth, refusing to show how much he was hurting me.

I shook my head, even though his question was rhetorical. Tonight, if not sooner, Arik was going to take out all his frustrations on me. The hold he had on my thigh was nothing compared to what was coming.

I'd ruined another of his opportunities by not letting the old, mangy wolf Arik wanted to do business with, fuck my mouth. The man had smelled of filth and rot. As soon as I'd opened my mouth, I'd vomited on his dick. That had been the end of that.

Arik's hand moved up and gripped my breast. He twisted it painfully in his palm and this time I yelped.

"Look at me when I'm talking to you, bitch." He pinched my nipple through the thin fabric of the short, low-necked black dress I wore, earning him another one of my pained noises before I could swallow the sound. I swore he thrived on them. He seemed to enjoy pushing me until I whimpered, which was why I held back as long as possible.

My gaze shot to his, but dropped immediately in submission to his Alpha wolf status. I was no match for his dominance. My kind of wolf had no rank within any pack.

"I've taken about as much of your shit as I can handle, Gem." He occasionally watched the one-lane gravel road we were on, a shortcut through the forest and over the mountains to wherever we were going next. We never stayed in one place for too long.

I murmured a halfhearted apology. No matter what I did now, Arik was going to punish me. I could take whatever he did, as I'd grown accustomed to his beatings over the past eight years or so.

Arik released his hold on me, placing both hands on the steering wheel, as he continued his rant. "I almost had him hooked. *All* you had to do..."

Tonight, he'd take out all his rage on me with his fists, then he'd gather me in his arms, clean me up, and fuck away all the pain. That was us. Our cycle. Over and over again until the end of our lives.

Was I proud of it? No. Did I know that it was a seriously fucked-up relationship? Yes.

But Arik had saved me, at least in the beginning. After I'd been shunned by my pack at fourteen, alone in the world for almost two long, rough years, he'd found me and took me in. It wasn't love, but he was all I had.

It was fine, except for the times when Arik let the monstrous side of himself out. When that happened... I tried my best to forget about it, though the scars I carried were a constant reminder. Or they would be if I let myself dwell on them. Instead, I pretended they didn't exist, or that someone else had given them to me.

My memories of those painful times played tricks on my brain sometimes. My recollection was fractured. It was easy to push it to the recesses of my mind, as I couldn't fully recall the details, so why try?

I preferred to think of Arik as my imperfect savior rather than as the monster who might one day cut me too deeply. He was all I had in this world. I knew after almost a decade with him that I couldn't survive on my own.

I was worthless without him. I needed his Alpha wolf to keep me safe, or the others would tear me apart.

"...next time. Gem, are you even listening to me?" A dangerous growl rumbled deep in his chest. That sound used to make me shake with fear. Now it fell flat, since I knew that when he was really angry and going to hurt me, he was quiet.

He would be quiet, almost serene tonight, before he dealt me my punishment.

"Of course I'm listening to you," I lied. I kicked off my heels and stretched my poor, aching toes. "You were talking about your next deal, since we lost that last one."

"And what was I saying about it? Who are we meeting with?" He intently watched me out of the corner of his eye.

"Um. Another potential client..." Honestly, I didn't give a shit about his scams, or who he was trying to con next. I was hungry and tired after leaving town in the middle of the night. The guy I'd thrown up on had looked at me like he wanted to snap my neck. His rage had turned on Arik, too. We couldn't stay there a moment longer without risking our lives.

"You fucking lying whore. You know what, that's it." His pupils shone with the golden light of his inner wolf. "I've taken care of you for *years*. I've given you everything and more. All I ask in return is that you use your body to help me out from time to time. You can't even do that one simple task, can you?"

I opened my mouth to reply when he reached across me and yanked the door handle.

Alarm widened my eyes. "What are you—?"

Without slowing down, he shoved me out the passenger door. I tried to reach for something, anything, but it all happened too fast.

I hit the ground and rolled. The gravel bit into my skin, soon giving way to hard packed pine needles on the forest floor. I coughed and sputtered, shocked that Arik would toss me out of a moving vehicle.

Moving gingerly to sit up, I stared after the dust left in the car's wake. Arik was long gone and this time, it didn't seem like he was coming back.

Shit.

I'd pushed him too far, and this time I was screwed. Unless... unless this was another one of his lessons.

The forest around me was strangely quiet and calm. No birds chirped, and a chill settled in the air. This was the middle of nowhere, and I was stuck here, potentially abandoned.

Climbing to my feet, I assessed my situation—no shoes, no coat, no purse, and miles from civilization. All I could do was wait and hope that Arik didn't leave me standing out here for too long.

I adjusted my dress, brushing away the debris. Scrapes and bruises showed on my forearms. My hip thudded with a dull ache where I must have landed on it, and the gravel had dug into my palms.

The seconds turned into minutes, and the minutes to nearly an hour. My feet went numb from standing on the frozen ground. Still, there was no sign of Arik.

He really left me and abandoned me in the middle of nowhere to die.

Panic crashed through my chest. I was going to die out here, alone in the woods, just like I'd always imagined would be my fate. It was the fate my pack wanted for me. It had simply been postponed while I lived on borrowed time with Arik.

I rubbed my bare shoulders. This dress barely covered my petite body. If it weren't for my meager wolf shifter abilities to heal from small wounds and generate an abundance of body heat, I would have died a long time ago. My first winter on the streets could have been my last.

The poorly maintained gravel road certainly saw little traffic, so it was pointless to wait for another vehicle to come by soon. I could follow the road back to town... We'd only been speeding along this route for a few hours. Though that angry guy and his cronies were there, so that seemed like a poor option. My only other choice was to try to find shelter in these woods.

As I stood pondering my options, my nose caught the faint scent of snow right before it started coming down in thick, puffy flakes. I gawked up at the sky. Whatever God controlled the weather was being particularly unkind to me today.

I scowled when the gentle fall of snow morphed into a full-on storm. The afternoon grew dark, forcing the sun to fully retreat, and the temperature plummeted.

Turning, I strode into the forest in search of shelter. The eerie quiet prickled my skin. This far up in the mountains, there should be animals, especially prey, even in the winter. But that wasn't the case here. Something was wrong with this woodland. Or, perhaps, larger, more aggressive predators had scared off the usual woodland creatures.

I shivered at the thought.

As I stumbled through the trees, I kept glancing over my shoulder. *Gem, focus.* I needed to find a cave, a hollow, anywhere to seek shelter from the worsening storm. My senses reached out as far as they could, but all I heard, smelled, and saw was the hushed forest and the piling snow.

The chill sank into my limbs, and I debated about

shifting to my wolf form. I hadn't shifted in years—hell, I didn't even know if I could anymore—when I spotted a faint light in the distance. I tipped my head back and caught a whiff of woodsmoke. There, through the trees and across a frozen stream, was a two-story cabin.

I stepped onto the covered porch and knocked. Hopefully, whoever lived here would take pity on a woman lost in the woods. Though if my tainted luck held true, they would let me inside, only to snare me in their net. For all I knew, a flesh-eating witch could live on this isolated mountain—or worse, bears.

Territorial, aggressive, unforgiving of intruders, bears were the worst kind of shifters. The last time Arik and I had a run-in with a bear, we'd barely escaped with our lives.

When no answer came, I knocked again. *Please, let this be my refuge.* I eyed the whirl of snowfall. It seemed to grow denser as I stood on the front step.

Again, there was no answer. I chewed on my thumbnail and frowned at the door, which separated me from warmth and shelter. The wind picked up, a frigid gust blowing my hair into my face.

The truth was, even in my wolf form, I was unlikely to make it through this blizzard alive without shelter. Plus, the lack of prey I came across worried me. Would I even find a meal in these woods? Or, if the elements didn't end me, would I eventually starve to death? I was certainly no skilled hunter.

A snow drift began to accumulate on the porch. I warily eyed it, and with a heavy sigh, made my decision.

I tried the door handle and found it unlocked. Holding my breath, I stepped inside the cabin and closed the door behind me.

"Hello?" I called, my voice echoing in the space.

2

GEM

I stood in a single open room that held a kitchen, a round dining table with seats for three, and three rocking chairs in front of the blazing hearth. Against the far wall was a staircase leading to the second floor. Did a family live here?

I glanced at the fireplace again. Who would leave the hearth burning like that when no one was home?

Cautiously, I stepped further into the room and parked myself in front of the fireplace. My feet began to tingle and itch as they warmed, and my nose leaked as it thawed. I sniffed. The bare bones furniture and decor told me little about whoever lived here.

Upon closer inspection of the flickering flames, I realized they burned evenly, and the fire had an unnatural tinge of blue and purple within the flame. The only way to describe it was... too perfect.

The hairs on the back of my neck stood on end.

Magic. Maybe I hadn't been too far off about assuming a flesh-eating witch lived here. Or worse—three witches.

For a second, I considered braving the storm rather than staying in a cabin where the hearth fire was fueled by magic. I took a deep breath, scenting the place, but all I could smell was a pleasant aroma that made me feel at home. It was probably a magical trick.

Visions from the tale of *Hansel and Gretel* popped to mind. Had this place magically lured me in so I could be cooked and eaten by woodland witches?

Pull it together. Witches only ate people in fairytales.

I turned to warm my backside, and my stomach grumbled as I now faced the kitchen area. Speaking of eating... Arik had wanted to get on the road immediately following that ruined business meeting. I didn't blame him, considering the threats they were hurling at us.

We'd gotten into the car and drove through the night. Having turned onto that gravel road *shortcut* that left civilization behind, there'd been no place to stop for breakfast or lunch.

Hunger pangs shot through my abdomen, and I gasped. It had been a while since I was this famished. Honestly, not since Arik found me beside a dumpster, munching away on a rat. Back then, I'd snarled at him, afraid that he was going to steal my only meal for the day. Instead, he took me and changed my life.

For better or for worse? Some days, it was one way more than the other.

I shook off the memories and crept to the kitchen, where the enormous refrigerator beckoned. Opening it, I found an abundance of food.

I'd already broken into this person's cabin. Would it really be that bad if I stole some food, too? Another spike of pain made me wrap my arms around my torso. When it passed, I grabbed some sliced meat and cheese, then found a loaf of fresh bread on the counter. Never mind making a sandwich, I tore off pieces of each and shoved them into my mouth.

Closing my eyes, I forced myself to thoroughly chew before swallowing. Eating too quickly never ended well, no matter how hungry you were.

Warm, filling my belly with delicious food, I softly moaned with contentment. Over the years, I'd learned to enjoy the little things, and the stolen moments when life was good—like this fleeting minute.

Honestly, breaking and entering—even though the door was unlocked—and stealing some food, were on the tamer side of the crimes I'd committed in order to survive.

As my stomach grew full, my eyelids began to droop. Arik had been so pissed off at me for last night's failure that he hadn't let me fall asleep in the car. His pinches, prods, and angry rants kept me up all night and throughout the day.

I glanced over at the three chairs in the living room, wondering why there was no other furniture, as I could have happily snoozed on a couch while waiting for the residents to return home, or for the storm to pass.

A door beside the kitchen caught my attention, but through it was just a bathroom.

My gaze drifted to the staircase and my feet followed. Upstairs was a short hallway with four doors, two on one side and one on the other, and the last at the far end.

I opened the first door and poked my head inside. The space was sparsely furnished, a similar style to downstairs, with a rustic-looking bed, wardrobe, and desk. My nose tickled as I inhaled the faint scent of honey, clove, and man.

A male witch? Possibly.

Closing the door, I moved on to the next one and found another man's room with a lot of heavy black furnishings inside. An earthy pine and lemon scent hit my nose.

The third door was locked. Strange, considering the front door had been unlocked. What were they hiding behind this one?

I moved on. The fourth room, while less mysterious, was certainly intriguing. Leather, cognac, and woodsmoke floated through my head, the scent masculine yet strangely comforting at the same time. A giant four-poster bed stood over a plush Persian carpet. Heavy drapes framed the windows at either side, and I was surprised to find a walk-in closet.

Three men, all living under the same roof... Strange? Why were they up here on this mountain in the middle of nowhere? So far, I couldn't tell if they were humans, witches, or shifters—or something else entirely.

Unease coiled around my ribcage. Human or supernatural, they were *men*. My experience with males wasn't the greatest, no matter the species.

I crossed the room and peeked out the window, only to see a dense whirl of white that obscured the view.

The reality was, I was trapped here until this stormed passed. Maybe I'd get lucky and the occupants wouldn't return until morning, and I could sneak out. It would be like I'd never been here at all.

I eyed the bed. Those sheets looked like satin. The plush comforter would be warm and soft. I could just lie down for a quick nap. That wouldn't hurt anything, would it?

The room's scent hit me again. It smelled so welcoming, almost beckoning me to make myself at home. Swaying on my feet, I decided to crawl into that bed before I passed out from exhaustion.

Fucking Arik. He'd left me in the woods to die. I'd be angrier about it if I wasn't so tired.

My head hit the fluffy pillow, that rich masculine scent surrounding me, wrapping me in its embrace. A tiny voice in my head screamed at me that something was horribly wrong, but I didn't have the strength to pay attention to it.

The last thought that went through my conscious mind was how much better this room smelled than any man I'd ever met, including Arik.

3
KEVIN

The wolf shifter pack howled and yipped in the distance, taunting us from across our territory's boundary. We'd had to chase them out twice in as many weeks. I stood on my hind legs, and drowned out their noise with a roar of my own, before coming down onto all fours and huffing at my two bear brothers.

If the wolves trespassed again, I was going to slaughter every last one of them. They knew the territory markers, and they simply didn't care. They purposely pissed on the trees on *our* side of the border, marking them as theirs. I was done playing games. If those stupid fucking wolves thought that we were just three nice bachelor bears who'd been born and raised in these woods, they were in for a surprise.

I hadn't worked my way up in Penumbra Syndicate only to retire and have to deal with this juvenile shit.

The *whole point* of coming to this forest, to our cabin, was for some damn peace and quiet. I was done with the bustle of the city. I'd earned my way out of the syndicate—well, as much *out* as someone could get.

I wanted us to deal with these wolf bastards on our own. But if we couldn't, then I'd have to call in a favor.

I inwardly cringed. I wanted peace, not another fucking turf war.

The sudden shift in weather caught my attention. *Snow.* I sniffed the air. No, not just snow, a storm was coming and it could well turn into a full-on blizzard. Blake and Nathaniel sensed it too; their noses pointed skyward. With a nod, the three of us turned to make the trek back to our cabin.

Just as I'd predicted, the snowfall soon swirled and battered against our thick fur as it gained intensity. I hoped it would be a terrible enough storm to do away with those wolf shifter pests. Maybe they'd freeze out here, and we'd finally be left in peace.

It wasn't out of the realm of possibility. This storm was coming in hard and fast.

Blake's black fur was visible enough as we lumbered home. However, I lost sight of Nathaniel's honey-blond pelt on multiple occasions as it blended with the whirling snowflakes. Luckily, our sense of direction was good.

By the time we arrived home, the sun had set, casting the world in a thick shadow of biting ice and wind. I couldn't wait to get inside, sit in my chair, and warm up in front of the ever-burning enchanted fire.

Having powerful friends came with certain perks, especially when those friends were witches and Fae who used magic.

We shifted on the front porch in order to fit through the cabin's door. If I were to build this place again, I would opt for a double door to accommodate our bear forms.

In companionable silence, we each dragged on a pair of black sweatpants that were folded in a cabinet by the entry. Clothing stashes were a necessity in a shifter's life. Not that being in the nude bothered any of us much. Still, I'd rather not sit around home with my dick hanging out. Nathaniel, Blake, and I were close—but not that kind of close.

I reached for a T-shirt, then paused when an unfamiliar scent drifted my way. Strawberries and a note of bright warmth, like sunshine, filled my nose.

Dropping my hand, I turned into the room and scrutinized the familiar surroundings. Nothing seemed out of place until I got to the kitchen. Crumbs littered the countertop like someone had been eating in that one spot and hadn't cleaned up after themselves. The fresh bread loaf was torn into, destroyed, like an animal had devoured it.

Annoyance shot through me. *Who the fuck was in our cabin?*

Blake nudged Nathaniel. "Do you smell that?"

Nathaniel nodded, his icy gaze scanning the room.

"Someone was here," I announced. However, another deep inhale told me a different story. "No. They are still here," I corrected myself. "Find them."

We fanned out, searching the main floor, not that there were too many places to hide. In unison, our attentions snapped to the stairs and our bedrooms on the second floor. Quietly, we crept up the steps.

Nathaniel opened his bedroom door, which was first in the hallway. Sure enough, the scent alone told us our intruder had been in here. We moved on to Blake's room and it told the same story. I tried my office door at the end of the hall, but it was still locked. A temporary relief eased the anger in my gut.

When we entered my room, we all stilled at the sight of a young woman with strawberry-blond hair sleeping in my bed. Her head rested on my pillow, her body under my blankets. Who the fuck was she?

My surprise was quickly replaced by irritation. On instinct, I inhaled her sweet, luring scent and my annoyance morphed into rage. *Wolf*. What the actual fuck?

By the matching scowls on my brothers' faces, I knew they'd identified what she was too. Nathaniel shot me a glacial stare, which told me just how pissed off he was at having a she-wolf invade our home.

Blake's lips pulled back, away from his teeth, in a snarl.

We approached my bed from all three sides in order to trap her once she woke. I wanted some fucking answers, and I was going to get them from this intruding wolf. Coming onto our lands was bad enough. But entering our house, our *home*, stealing our food, and defiling my bed? That was a death sentence.

That wolf pack had to know that we would skin this

bitch alive. Why would they send one of their own to such a death?

I needed answers. *Now.*

4

GEM

I woke with a small gasp and lay perfectly still. What had disturbed my sleep? An eerie silence hung in the air, like a weight pressing down on my body and smothering my senses. An unnatural cold pressed against my skin. My stomach was tangled in knots, but I couldn't point to why.

Then I heard it again—a trio of low, threatening growls.

Bolting upright, I pressed my back against the plush headboard and stared into three pairs of furious eyes. The owners of those eyes were the largest men I'd ever seen. So tall that they towered over me like mountains, menacing and snarling. Their enormous shoulders made the large bedroom feel cramped.

I quickly assessed them. They wore black cloth pants and their chests were bare. One of them had full sleeve tattoos, and another had so much ink there was barely a patch of skin left unmarked. The third, and oldest of them, looked twice as dangerous, even though he wore a solo tattoo—a circle within a circle on his chest.

I stared back at them, paralyzed with fear. My breath came in shallow pants.

The older one growled again, and the sound was pure animal. Then, I saw the unnatural glint in his eyes, the elongating of his canines, and his terrifying size, and it suddenly made sense. *Bear shifter.*

I was so fucked.

Bears were notoriously territorial. They were going to rip me to shreds just for being here. When I thought of how I'd eaten their food and *slept* in one of their beds... What had I been thinking?

A soft, wolfish whine sounded in my throat, which only seemed to anger them more. How had I not scented them as soon as I entered their den? I really was the weakest of wolves. Worthless. No wonder Arik had ditched me.

Even now, when I inhaled, their scent floated pleasantly through my nose. This was wrong, all wrong. They had an enchanted fireplace. Maybe they were somehow magically hiding their scents, too, which would mean they knew a witch.

How much worse could this get?

"What are you doing in *my bed*?" The older bear somehow seemed to grow larger as he glared down at me. His hazel eyes burned with rage.

I swallowed hard. My pulse whooshed in my ears, sounding too loud inside my head. "I-I—"

The tattoo-covered bear shifter reached out,

wrapped my hair around his fist, and yanked me from the bed. I yelped at the sudden pain in my scalp, but that sensation was soon forgotten as his presence enveloped me. He tugged my back against his chest, one hand in my hair and the other around my waist to hold me in place. His heat seared my skin through the thin fabric of the dress I still wore, and my nose filled with his pine and citrus scent.

Everything about him was overwhelming, intoxicating, and dangerous. Yet—alluring. I trembled against him.

"I said, what are you doing in my bed?" the older bear asked.

My gaze latched onto him as he approached, pure predator in the bunch and roll of his muscles. His hazel eyes had deepened to a brown so dark they were nearly black. His gaze bored right through me, laying me bare before him.

I whimpered, melting back into the wall of heat and muscle behind me. I only had two options—shift, and piss them off, as I put up a pathetic fight before I tried to run. Even if I weren't *me*, one wolf against three bears was unwinnable odds.

Or I could beg for mercy and hope they set me free. Hell, I'd take the blizzard over these three enormous men. I never should have fallen asleep.

I mentally reached inside, searching for my wolf. If she was in there, she remained still and silent, no help at all. I was on my own.

"Don't make me repeat myself a third time." He roughly cupped my jaw in one massive hand and forced me to look up at him. Brown hair with touches of gray showed his age. "I don't like to repeat myself."

I licked my dry lips. "I-I was stranded, and then the storm... I saw your cabin and thought—"

"You thought you could enter our home, steal our food, and soil *my bed* with your filth!" he roared, and I flinched. "You invaded our space, took what was not yours, and you will pay for your crimes."

"Kevin, maybe we should—" The floorboards creaked as the third bear, who had tousled-blond hair, moved closer to us.

"Don't fucking interrupt me!" Kevin snarled.

My wide, horrified eyes darted to the blond man's cold green glare. Something warm briefly flickered in his gaze before they frosted over again. He clamped his mouth shut, his jaw ticking. The faint hope I had of him intervening died a quick death. I'd get no help from him.

"I'm sorry," I whispered.

Kevin, who seemed to be their leader, leaned in, his breath hot across my face as he said, "*Sorry* isn't good enough." Then he stepped away and ran his fingers through his gray-streaked brown hair, his gaze never leaving mine.

The bear who held me immobile chuckled darkly in my ear. "We chased your wolf shifter friends out of our territory, so don't expect anyone to come rescue you."

"What are you talking about?" My brow bunched with confusion. "I'm not part of any pack. I didn't even know there were other wolves—"

"Don't lie." Kevin's fury had calmed, which somehow made him scarier than when he was livid. His gaze openly swept over me, taking in my bare feet, scuffs, and the tiny, clingy dress. "If they thought we'd go easier on their pack whore, they were greatly mistaken. Why are you here? To seduce us?" He sneered as if I repulsed him. "Do you bring a message from your pack?"

Panic curled tight around my lungs and squeezed. For a long moment, I couldn't breathe. How was I supposed to convince them I had nothing to do with this other pack, when they'd already made up their minds about who I was and what I was doing here?

I gave a small shake of my head. "I don't know anything about that pack. I swear. Please believe me. Please let me go."

"She's pretty when she begs, isn't she?" the bear shifter behind me said. His arm around my waist tightened like an iron bar. A fresh wave of panic seized me.

What were they going to do to me if I couldn't convince them I had no wicked agenda? Did they even care about the truth?

Based on my experiences, men thrived on two things—violence and sex.

The third bear's glare deepened at the one standing behind me. "She's telling the truth."

Hope unfurled in my chest again as Kevin seemed to consider the blond's words. "Are you sure, Nathaniel? She could be trying to deceive us."

The blond, Nathaniel, slowly nodded. "Positive. Absolutely positive."

He must have some special kind of power to know when a person was lying or telling the truth. Supernaturals were especially difficult to read, yet Nathaniel was certain, and Kevin took his word for it.

He surprised me by saying, "Blake, let her go."

I finally had a name for the last bear in this room. Blake tightened his hold on me and I grunted at the pain. He was going to crush my spine and tear out my hair.

"I thought we were going to punish her," he said, his words sending a spike of fear straight through me. He spoke in my ear, "I'd like to bend you over my knee and spank that pert little ass of yours."

I shook with a tremble that had nothing to do with fear. I should have found his words repulsive, but I didn't. At least not entirely. His citrusy pine scent was heady, and I swore it was messing with my brain and my body the longer he held me against him.

Ugh, I had the worst taste in men.

"Oh, she will be punished," Kevin assured him. His tone hardened. "Let. Her. Go."

Blake slowly released me and took one step back. I was free, yet still caged in by three huge men. They'd made up their mind to make me pay, but I wasn't sure what form that would take yet.

I glanced over my shoulder at Blake, taking in his striking blue eyes and shoulder-length black hair. His features contrasted Nathaniel's blond hair and paler skin. They were each stunning in their own way. Lethal and terrifying too, yet I couldn't seem to keep my eyes from drifting to their bare chests, their tattoos, and their intense eyes.

Anticipation grew thick in the air as they all stared back at me.

Kevin cleared his throat, gaining my attention. "What's your name?"

"Gem." I hugged my middle.

"Gem, you have a choice to make," he said in a flat, detached tone. "Either we kill you now for your crimes, or we toss you outside and you can take your chances in this storm, or…"

I hung onto his every word. "Or?" I prompted.

"Or," his gaze flitted to Nathaniel's, then Blake's, before resting on me again. "Or you atone for your crimes by being ours for three months."

I blinked up at him. "What do you mean by being… yours?"

"Exactly what it sounds like." Kevin advanced on me, his strides slow and deliberate. "You will do everything we ask of you willingly and without complaint."

I retreated, stepping backward until I bumped into Blake's solid chest again. He rested his massive palms on my shoulders. Strangely, I couldn't decide if the embrace was menacing or comforting. *Of course it's menacing.*

"What kinds of things?" I asked, my gaze searching Kevin's, which had returned to a hazel brown. Option number one was a no-go. Who would choose immediate death when there were other options?

Before, I might have thought that I'd rather be outside, taking my chances in the storm than whatever these three had in store for me, but on second thought,

I'd changed my mind. I wasn't going to choose death by snowstorm either. I didn't hate myself *that* much.

But this other option... it made my heart pound and my skin flush. I should be terrified of these three, and especially of what they were proposing, but as their scents mingled and filled the space, I couldn't think straight.

One second, I felt chilled to the bone by their dangerous presence, and the next, I wanted to sink into them as if I'd found my way home.

I knew I was fucked up, but this was a whole new level. Alarm bells rang through my mind as I tried to get a grasp on reality. They were my captors, my enemy, and if I made it out of this alive, I'd probably wish I were dead.

Kevin caught my chin between his forefinger and thumb. "You will do anything and everything we ask of you. No boundaries and no limitations. Willingly."

"For three months? Then I'm free to go after that?" I clarified.

"Yes. That's the deal." He searched my face.

My gaze flicked to Nathaniel's stony expression, then back to Kevin's rich hazel eyes. What would they want of me? He *had* called me a pack whore. Is that what they wanted, someplace to shove their cocks? A female to warm their beds at night?

Men were so fucking predictable. All these assholes were the same.

"There's one thing I don't understand," I said. "Why would you want to keep me here with you? You made it very clear that you hate wolf shifters. Why keep me in your house?"

"Punishment, remember?" Kevin swept his thumb across my bottom lip. "I'd never put someone I actually liked through what I have in mind for you."

My breath hitched. It seemed my life was on track for more of the same brutality. These assholes could do their worst. I didn't care anymore.

After a long silence, I said, "Okay. I'll do it."

Maybe I did hate myself.

On the other hand, whatever they wanted from me couldn't possibly be worse than the things I'd done for Arik. He'd bartered with my body on numerous occasions. Some of the men who'd had me for a night were sick fucks.

These three bears? I could take whatever they threw at me. I guaranteed that I had already survived worse. I'd survive them too.

Then in three months' time, I'd be free. Free to... what? Sink back into the slums, dumpster diving for my next meal? Or become a feral in the woods? Either way, this chapter of my life would be over.

Life was full of shitty options and shittier options. Take your pick.

5

GEM

Contradictory to my expectations, sex seemed to be the furthest thing from their minds. I thought I'd been agreeing to let them use my body for pleasure, but that was not it at all. No, they wanted me to do chores. And when I wasn't busy doing chores, the name of the game was degradation.

That first night set the tone for what was to come. They ate dinner and tossed scraps on the floor for me—like I was a dog. Humiliated but hungry, I ate every morsel. I was eventually given a single threadbare blanket and told to sleep on the floor in front of the fireplace. At least it was warm, and way more comfortable than any alleyway.

Sleep that night was fleeting as I lay awake until the early hours of the morning, listening to the storm rage outside. What was to become of me? How had I made even more of a mess of my life?

In a way it was a relief to know that I had three

months here with a roof over my head. Even if I was only fed scraps on the floor, at least it was a consistent food source. But after this, what would I do and where would I go?

It was a wolf-eat-wolf world out there, and mine had gone silent years ago.

Finally, my eyelids stayed closed and sleep claimed me for what must have been a few hours, even though it felt like mere minutes, before I was rudely woken by a bucket of ice water splashed across my body.

I shot upright and sputtered. Icy rivulets trickled down my skin. My damp hair clung to my face and shoulders, and I shivered.

"Wake up, princess!" Blake bellowed, the empty bucket in hand. He chuckled and tossed a chunk of bread on the wet floor. "Eat."

I snatched up my breakfast and glared at him.

He chuckled again. "Keep looking at me like that, princess, and I will bend you over my knee."

I dropped my gaze, then glanced around the room. "Where are the other two?"

"Out. The storm has settled a bit." He toed me with his boot. "It's just you and me today. You have work to do. Get up."

A chill crawled up my spine at the thought of being alone with Blake. Kevin wasn't here to curb his behavior. I would have preferred Nathaniel's icy stares to Blake's heated threats.

"What am I supposed to do?" I rose to my feet and brushed the wet strands of hair out of my face.

"For starters, clean the cabin. I want it spotless by

this afternoon. Those are Kevin's orders." Blake settled into one of the three rocking chairs. Today, he wore jeans and a sweater, his long dark hair tied at the nape of his neck. "You can start by cleaning up this floor. All that water's not good for the hardwood."

I barely suppressed the urge to glare at him again. Never mind that *he* was the one who'd soaked the floor —and me.

I found a wash bucket, mop, and several rags, among basic cleaning supplies in the kitchen closet. On my hands and knees, I sopped up the water and wrang it out into the bucket, repeating the process until the floor was dry. All the while, Blake rocked in his chair and watched—more like stared the whole time.

Ugh, what a creeper.

Standing, I placed my hands on my hips and faced him. "Is that clean enough for you?"

Blake lifted a dark brow, and I regretted my sassy remark. One of his long legs shot out and sent the bucket of dirty water flying across the room. It hit the wall, spewing its contents everywhere.

I gaped at him in utter disbelief.

"Get on your knees and clean that up," he rumbled, his eyes flashing with heat.

Fury unwound in my chest as my cheeks grew hot. What a fucking asshole.

I had to remind myself that I'd trespassed on their land, stolen from them, and this was my punishment. I was guilty, even if I'd been desperate and had no other choice.

As promised, I'd do whatever they wanted without

complaint. So, I dropped to my hands and knees and cleaned the floor—again.

After I'd cleaned up the second bucket of spilled water, Blake insisted that I scrub the floor with a soft bristled brush. By the time afternoon rolled around, my knees were bruised, my hands chaffed, and every muscle in my body ached. But the floor shone. It had probably never been this clean before.

With a groan, I climbed to my feet and rubbed my lower back. If I were a normal wolf, by tomorrow, my body would heal, and I'd be good as new to continue to take this type of punishment. But I wasn't a normal wolf. My body didn't work right. Not that I was going to tell him that. It was my secret to keep.

Blake strode from the kitchen, where he'd made himself lunch, into the living room to sit in his chair again. He ate messily, flinging honey and breadcrumbs all over my freshly washed floor.

I clenched my teeth, waiting for him to finish, then resumed cleaning up his mess.

He smirked down at me, refusing to move as I cleaned. The scent of sweet honey made my empty stomach rumble with hunger. The scrap of bread I'd had for breakfast was long gone.

I tidied up as best I could with him in my way, but before I could stand again, Blake dropped his plate on the floor. It shattered into a million tiny pieces.

"Oops," he drawled, sounding anything but apologetic.

I couldn't stop the snarl that escaped my throat. I'd taken enough of his shit.

Blake's blue eyes glimmered with amusement. "You want to fight, wolf-girl? Go ahead and shift. Show me what you got. I'll even give you one free pass to sink those canines and claws into me, princess."

I slowly rose, maintaining eye contact with him. He remained seated, not even seeing me as enough of a threat to get the fuck up from his rocking chair. I couldn't exactly blame him. At five-foot-nothing inches, even standing to my full height, I was eye to eye with him while he was sitting down. He'd have to be on the floor in order for me to be able to look down on the fucker.

A growl rumbled in my chest. I was exhausted and pissed off. This was day one, and honestly, I wasn't sure I was going to make it for the entire three months. At some point, I really was going to wish that I was dead. Or, I'd just drop from sheer exhaustion.

Blake reached out and wrapped his fingers around my neck. I startled, stumbling as he pulled me close. "You either show me your wolf and take a shot at me, or get this mess cleaned up." He squeezed, making me gasp and claw at his hands. "Which will it be?"

I stood zero chance of fighting him in my wolf or human form. Trying to shift would only humiliate me further. If I managed it, he'd see my true nature, and why my birth pack rejected me. I couldn't stand that level of humiliation.

Heat burned behind my eyes, but there was no way in hell I was going to cry in front of this beastly asshole. I bit the inside of my cheek until my tongue tasted the metallic tang of blood. Only then did I trust myself to speak.

"I'll clean." My voice came out steady and even.

Blake's hold on my neck relaxed, but he didn't let go. He dipped his nose to my hair and deeply inhaled, startling me. "You smell like strawberries and honey. I've never liked the smell of wolf so much. I could eat you up."

Panic chilled me to the core. He pulled back far enough to meet my gaze, and I saw the glint of his bear within. His canines began to elongate, his fingernails grew into claws...

Blake stood so abruptly that his chair slid backward. He released me with a snarl, strode out the front door, and slammed it shut.

I stared after him, my breath coming in rapid, shallow bursts. What had just happened? Did his bear really want to... eat me?

6

BLAKE

The wolf-girl, Gem, was outside stacking firewood, barefoot and wearing nothing but that fucking little, tiny dress. Not that it mattered, wolves were hardy creatures. Like most other types of vermin, they were difficult to kill, much less seriously injure. Shifters of all types were quick healers. I'd have to push her much harder to cause her any real discomfort or pain.

I was still warming up to my role as punisher. I'd push her harder soon.

For now, I was enjoying watching her work on her hands and knees. I was going out of my way to get her on all fours. Hell, I was having dreams about her sweet ass. I was going to drive myself crazy, so today I had to get her out of the house.

The storm from two nights ago had subsided, but another was blowing in this evening.

"Where do you think she came from, if she's not

part of that wolf pack in the area?" I asked Nathaniel. He insisted she was telling the truth about not being affiliated with them, and not even knowing about their existence, but if that was true... then who the fuck was she? Scantily clad wolf shifter girls didn't just appear in the middle of the woods.

I knew for a fact I was living a wet dream, because Kevin had made it very clear that none of us were allowed to fuck her. I wasn't a total brute, I would have made it good for her too. Even so, the boss said *no* and his word was law in this cabin.

"Maybe one of you should ask her," Nathaniel grunted as he whittled a chunk of wood into what looked like some sort of animal. He'd been particularly standoffish, and distracted, since the girl arrived. I couldn't tell what was bothering him, but something certainly was on his mind. When he was ready to talk about it, he would. Until then, I'd give him space.

We sat in our rocking chairs in front of the glowing fireplace, enjoying a peaceful, quiet evening. Now that the girl was doing all the chores around here, we were free to more efficiently patrol our lands each day. Of course one of us had to keep an eye on her, to oversee her punishment, but that barely qualified as work. I'd volunteered to do it.

I enjoyed my work most days, except for the fact that my bear kept snarling at me when I made a new mess for her to clean up. I had no idea what was up with that. He was restless, sullen, and a total killjoy.

The wolf-girl deserved to be *punished*, and that's what I was dishing out. None of it would cause her life-long damage. She was a wolf shifter for fuck's sake. Sure, we might have scared her a bit in the beginning, when we were angry. I frowned, thinking back on how I'd held her neck and almost bitten her the other day. Fear and panic had rolled off her in waves.

My inner bear roared at the memory, slamming against my ribcage. I pushed it away. A little fear was good for her. We didn't want her getting complacent, or worse, thinking she could run away without consequence.

Weirdly, at the thought of her running off, possessiveness curled around my insides. My inner bear growled. She was mine—ours. She wasn't going anywhere, at least not for the next three months. Though that also seemed too soon.

Hell, the loneliness out here must be getting to me if I'm feeling possessive of a fucking wolf-girl who invaded our space.

Kevin's chair creaked, snapping me out of my thoughts. "I don't care where she came from," he said. His lie hung heavy in the air. I could taste it, and so could Nathaniel, who popped his head up at leveling his assessing gaze on Kevin.

I snorted. "Bullshit. You probably had your Penumbra Syndicate friends run a full background check on her. You were head of their security before you retired. Don't pretend like you're not all over this mystery she-wolf. We know you better than that."

Kevin shot me a glare that would make lesser men shit their pants and cower. Luckily for him—I inwardly grinned—I wasn't that type. I met his glower with a knowing smirk.

So far he'd done his best to ignore Gem. His overt disinterest spoke volumes of just how intrigued he was by her. We'd lived together long enough to know each other quite well. Secrets didn't last long around here.

"So," I said. "What have you got on her? Who is she?"

Kevin shook his head. "There's no record matching her name and appearance in the wolf shifter database. No record of her attending any academy either. They're still looking though."

"I have an idea. We could interrogate her until she tells us everything," I suggested. The chores as punishment were Kevin's idea, and it was fine. But I still itched to get my hands on her and show her another form of punishment. Watching her on her hands and knees for the past few days, her pert little ass up in the air, was driving me crazy.

I longed to spank her until she was soaking wet and begging for my cock. If I had her enthusiastic permission, then surely Kevin wouldn't mind if I banged her, right? My hand in the shower was getting old.

Kevin sighed but agreed to my idea to question her. "Fine. We don't need a stranger, and potential unknown threat, living under our roof. Bring her in here. Let's see if she will tell the truth."

Nathaniel continued to stare at his whittling project. Was he even listening to us? I assumed not, so I took it upon myself to fetch the she-wolf.

Outside, the evening air was frigid. My breath

clouded, and snow crunched under my boots as I strolled toward the woodshed behind our cabin. Gem was working away, stacking firewood just like I'd shown her earlier. As I drew closer to her, I felt a magnetic pull, as if I couldn't alter course if I'd tried.

Her rose gold hair hung to her waist, swaying from her movements. She panted and grunted as she heaved heavy logs into place. For such a little thing, she was unrelenting, seeing each chore through to its end without complaint. Even now, when she had to lift onto her toes to reach the top of the stack, she did it without grumbling. Such a good girl.

"Hey, princess." I kept my tone light.

She whirled around so fast, she lost her balance and stumbled right into my chest. I gripped her arm to steady her, and that small contact stole my breath away for several long moments. She gazed up at me with wide blue eyes, so deep and rich that I could get lost in them.

I *wanted* to get lost in them. My gaze found her lush lips, parted with shallow breaths that fogged in the air. My bear perked up and pushed me toward her. All I had to do was lean down and claim...

She took a step back, breaking the spell. "Why are you sneaking up on me?" she accused.

I shook off the haze that had clouded my mind. My gaze dropped to her peaked nipples, clearly outlined through that dress. A possessive snarl caught in my throat. It was a good thing we were in the middle of the woods because the mere thought of another man, an outsider, seeing her tits like that made me feel murderous.

My eyes traveled lower, taking in the bruises on her knees. My brow pinched, all lust vanishing, and was replaced with confusion. She was a shifter. Those should have healed by now.

Filing that thought away, I said, "We need you inside. Come on."

Reluctantly, she followed me inside the cabin, her expression wary. I left her to stand before us and retook my seat. My skin prickled at the awareness of Kevin's and Nathaniel's eyes on her. I had to stop myself from rising and covering her up.

A heavy silence descended on us. The crackle of the fire was the only sound. Gem chewed on the inside of her cheek, nervously shifting her weight from one foot to the other.

Finally, Kevin spoke. "My people can't find any information on you, so you're going to have to tell us who you are and where did you come from?"

Gem's gaze flitted between me and Kevin. Nathaniel ignored her, working his blade into the wood, so she did the same to him.

"I... My boyfriend and I got into a fight and he left me along the side of the gravel road that runs through these woods."

Boyfriend? Red momentarily blazed across my vision. *Mine.* The word popped into my head and I had to fight down the desire to leave right now and hunt down the man who'd not only touched her, but who'd abandoned her in the wilderness.

Shaking off the urge, I asked, "You mean the old logging road?" That was a treacherous path in the best of seasons. In winter, it was nearly impassable. Any stupid tourist who thought it was a shortcut was often found dead in the spring.

Gem shrugged. "I don't know, I guess. It's not too far from here."

From here, no. But it was a long way from everywhere else, just as we were. And her *boyfriend* had abandoned her at the side of it? Motherfucker.

A strange, prickly sensation crept through my gut and twisted.

"Do you have ID on you?" Kevin asked.

"No. I left my purse in the car."

Kevin grunted. "Where are your shoes?"

"Also in the car."

"He didn't let you take any of your belongings?" I asked, confused.

Gem's gaze dropped to the floor. "He sort of... threw me out of the car while it was still moving. I didn't have a chance to get my things."

The heat coursing through me intensified, and red haze haloed my vision again. The fucker did *what*? I was going to kill him, slowly and painfully. My fingers clenched into fists.

Since I met her, I wasn't being especially nice to Gem, but she was being punished for a reason. It wasn't my role to be kind to her. She'd made her choices and now she had to deal with the consequences. Fair was fair.

H story made me think that maybe her intentions hadn't been nefarious after all. Had it been horrible timing, and bad luck, that we'd come across her when we were furious over the wolf shifters encroaching on our territory? Could she really be a lost, rejected wolf-girl who'd needed food and shelter?

My gut wrenched.

Kevin cleared his throat. "I see." How the fuck was he so calm right now? "Where do you come from?"

"A small family pack in Canada," she answered in a small voice. I could tell that she hated talking about her family. Though she hid it well, her tone betrayed a soul-deep hurt.

"What did they do to you?" I asked, leaning forward, and she startled at my question—or perhaps it was my low, lethal tone of voice.

"Um."

"The truth," Nathaniel said, speaking for the first time. His gaze settled over her and I could tell he was studying her as intensely as both Kevin and I were.

Gem squirmed under our combined scrutiny. "They banished me from the pack."

"Why?" Kevin's voice was quiet, soothing, as if she were a frightened animal who might flee, and he *wasn't* the big, bad bear who'd hunt her down. I doubted he was fooling anybody.

The she-wolf shook her head. "For reasons I'd rather not get in to. Let's just say, I wasn't good enough for them. The Keely pack couldn't deal with a disgrace like me."

The Keely pack. I made a mental note of that name.

"What about your parents?" Kevin asked.

She fidgeted. "My father is the pack Alpha. It was his decision to cast me out when I was fourteen."

The fury inside me continued to grow with each word she uttered.

"And your mother?"

"She always sided with my father. Our pack was at war and they couldn't afford any weakness. The only person who didn't want me to go was my younger sister, Jewels. But she was only seven, so she didn't get a say."

I looked her up and down—again. What didn't her pack like about her? She was gorgeous, in a petite, wolfish kind of way. I didn't sense any *weakness* in her.

"Tell me about your boyfriend," Kevin said, leaning forward and steepling his fingers. "His name, occupation, everything."

Gem licked her lips and hugged herself in a defensive pose. "Arik Asher is his name. He, um, is in business for himself."

I exchanged a glance with Nathaniel. What was that supposed to mean? It sounded like he was doing some illegal shit.

Kevin apparently came to the same conclusion. "Theft, blackmail, or con artist? What does he do, Gem?"

She sighed, seeming resigned to our questioning. "All of it. Anything to make a buck, and I mean anything. He doesn't have a lot of scruples, if any."

The fire in me turned into an inferno. Before I could stop myself, I asked, "What was your part in his schemes?"

She folded in on herself, her gaze locked on the floor again. "I helped sometimes."

I stood, closing the distance between us, my muscles bunched with tension. I circled my fingers around her slender neck and forced her to meet my gaze. I wanted to look into her eyes when she answered me next. "Did he ever make a buck off of you?"

Her soft blue eyes flashed with panic, then hurt, and finally humiliation. I felt her hard swallow beneath my palm.

"Yes." She spoke the single word so softly I barely heard it. "But I owed him. For taking care of me."

I tamped down on my rage before it completely consumed me. Leaning down, I spoke into her ear, "I don't care if he fucking saved your life ten times over. He had no right to sell your body." I growled, and she shivered beneath my touch.

After Gem fell asleep that night, we sat on the front porch. I stared out at the snow flurries, trying to shove my anger back into its box. It turned out Gem was not what we'd expected. We'd assumed she was a spy, or at the very least, a distraction sent to keep us busy while that nuisance of a wolf pack came up with a new plan to take our land.

Instead, she was nothing more than a girl lost in the woods, seeking shelter from a deadly blizzard. Were we wrong to punish her?

No. She'd still stolen our food, invaded our privacy, and crawled into Kevin's bed. This was our sanctuary.

Bear shifters didn't take lightly to intruders, and we were no exception.

"You're absolutely certain everything she said was true?" I asked Nathaniel, again.

He released a long-suffering sigh. "For the millionths time, yes."

I believed him. He was our very own shifter lie detector. Before coming to live with us, he'd made a name for himself as an interrogator. He was the best of the best. Just the mention of his name made some people fall apart and confess. It was impressive.

"What are we going to do with her?" I asked Kevin.

The older bear puffed on his pipe, releasing smoke rings into the crisp night air. "For now, she's ours to punish, and protect, as we see fit."

Nathaniel grunted. "We should send her away. No good will come of keeping her around for any longer."

"No," I snarled at him. "You can keep ignoring her if you want, but she's..." I trailed off, trying to ignore the growly, possessive feeling in my gut. I didn't know what the fuck was going on, but that little she-wolf set my bear on edge. He was restless these days, unable to stay away from her, or to stop thinking about her. My fingers curled into fists in my lap. I ached to touch her soft skin. The desire was becoming too much. It was becoming an obsession.

"She's what?" Nathaniel prompted, his unsettling green eyes boring into mine. "What is she to you?"

I shrugged. "Nothing. I don't know." I needed to get myself, and my bear, under control. Or maybe giving in to temptation was the only way to get her out of my system. Damn Kevin for making her off-limits.

Nathaniel stood, sneering down at me. "You're a fool." With those words, he let himself into the cabin, and went upstairs to his room.

"Rude," I muttered. Glancing over at Kevin, I asked, "What's his problem?"

Kevin seemed lost in thought, his focus on that damn pipe.

What was wrong with everyone around here lately? One woman shows up in our house and suddenly we're all losing our minds.

7
GEM

"Rise and shine, princess." Blake's deep voice woke me with a jolt. I groaned and rolled over beneath my threadbare blanket. Outside, the storm continued to howl, so all three bears were gathered around the table this morning. I felt self-conscious waking to their piercing gazes.

I'd hoped all of last night's confessions on my part would earn me at least some sympathy, but from the looks of things, that wasn't the case. If anything, their expressions had hardened.

Blake loomed over me, a twinkle of mischief in his blue eyes that gave me pause. What was he up to now? So far, he'd been the only one to stay in the cabin with me while the other two were out doing whatever it was they did. Over the past few days, I'd gotten to know Blake "the Asshole" rather well.

"You need a shower." He scanned my body. "You're a

filthy little wolf." That last part came out on a low growl, and his eyes heated enough to make me blush.

Gah, I hated how my body reacted to his gravelly voice and lustful eyes. I saw how he watched me clean and do other chores. Some stupid part of me liked it, was lured in by the hope of feeling wanted. Another part of me seethed, whispering in the back of my mind about how pathetic I was, and reminded myself that these bears were my enemy.

All they wanted was their pound of flesh, then they'd dump me back out into the world like I wasn't their damn problem anymore.

I stood up and yawned. Another day of discomfort surely lay ahead.

Blake stepped closer and surprised me by taking my arm and tossing me over his shoulder. I let out a startled cry.

"What are you doing?" I demanded, my fists pounding on his back.

"Giving you what you need, princess."

When he moved toward the bathroom door, my cheeks flamed as realization dawned. He was taking me in there to bathe.

He closed the door behind us and set me on the sink vanity. The space was relatively generous in size considering how small the cabin was in general. Even so, with Blake's large frame so near, I felt like I couldn't move. There was certainly no escaping whatever form of punishment, or humiliation, he had in mind this morning.

Giving you what you need. *What did that mean? A shower?*

I steeled myself, ready for anything. Or so I thought.

He wrapped one hand around the back of my neck, the hold purely possessive and dominating, while his other hand slipped under the shoulder strap of my dress.

"We own you," he said. "You agreed to that for three months."

I scoffed, the sound cut short as his hold tightened on my neck. "I had no other choice," I reminded him.

"You could have braved the storm."

"And probably would have died. No thank you."

"You could have tried to run away." His thumb brushed over my pulse.

I faltered. "You would have hunted me down."

"True." A soft smile played across his lips. "It was still a choice that you made. Now you have to live with your decision." His warm breath washed across my face. "Take your clothes off. I want to look at you."

"No." My breath hitched as I surprised myself by refusing him. "If you want to fuck me, you can do it with my clothes on."

Apparently, that had been the wrong thing to say. Blake's eyes flamed, then cooled as they filled with curiosity. His dark brows knitted as he studied me. "I'm not going to fuck you." He squinted. "What are you hiding?"

"Nothing." Even to my ears that sounded like a lie, but I hadn't had sex nude since... Well, for a long time.

Even Arik preferred to bend me over, fully clothed, and fuck me from behind.

"Liar." Blake's tone chilled me. "If you don't take off this dress, I'll tear it to shreds."

My pulse spiked, and anxiety crawled across my skin. I believed him.

It's okay.

He'll see, then he'll leave me alone. He won't want me.

Unless he wants to add to the menagerie, a tiny voice spoke in the back of my mind.

I was really starting to hate that pesky little voice. She said the absolute worst things.

Yet again, I had to choose between two shitty options. I could either let him take what he wanted, or I could give it to him.

So, I took back some of the control and slid off the vanity to stand in front of him. With a cold numbness overtaking my mind, I slid the straps over my shoulders and peeled the dress from my body. Straightening up, I stepped out of it, leaving myself completely bare.

Blake's eyes flashed with fiery desire as he took me in. His gaze scorched my skin, leaving a trail of heat on my flesh.

I could see the moment he found what I'd been hiding. His lust cooled, and he blinked hard, twice. A frown tugged at his generous mouth. Instead of turning away, like I'd expected, he reached out. His feather light touch on my arm sent a blast of heat right between my thighs.

Why wasn't he turning away in horror? Or sneering with disgust? Or laughing?

His fingers slid from my arm to my abdomen, leaving a searing trail in their wake. He first traced the claw mark scar that raked across my stomach. Then he found each cigar burn that peppered my skin. Those, he circled with his thumb. His touch was so light and warm that it almost tickled.

Lastly, his finger grazed the horizontal knife cuts that left pale lines on the front of my thighs. Some were deeper than others, some older, but the newest were a paler pink.

The tiny hairs on my skin stood on end, hypersensitive to his touch, while I closed my mind to this humiliating situation. I clenched my jaw and continued to stand rigidly before him, my hands fisted at my sides, as he made his languid exploration.

"Look at me." It was a command.

Hesitantly, I dragged my gaze from his chest up to his burning blue eyes. Instead of lust, they were filled with so much rage that I involuntarily took a step back.

Blake followed my retreat, pinning me between him and the bathroom's tiled wall. My heart hammered in my chest. Was he angry at me? Why? What had I done?

I shivered when his thumb traced the claw marks again. My stomach did a strange kind of flip-flop.

"Who did this to you?" His voice was laced with both compassion and danger.

As I searched his eyes, realization dawned. He wasn't upset *with* me, he was upset *for* me. A ragged mix of indiscernible emotions bombarded me.

My mental shields all but shattered. Awareness of the moment slammed into me so hard that my head spun. I drew in one rapid breath after another, my chest rising and falling in quick succession. Still, I couldn't breathe.

I couldn't answer his question either. That one simple question threatened to summon the shadows, to unlock the horrors that I'd contained in the recesses of my mind for years. I couldn't—I just couldn't—

"Gem?" Blake wrapped me in his arms and pulled me into his chest. "*Fuck*," he quietly cursed, almost to himself. "Princess, it's okay. I've got you. No one is going to lay a finger on you or I'll fucking kill them. You hear me? You're safe now."

In that moment, Blake "the Asshole" seemed to step aside for this different version of himself. One that saw into my soul. This tender, protective Blake was not one I'd met before. As I inhaled his citrus pine scent, a small part of me believed him when he swore I was safe.

Blake left me to shower on my own. He took my filthy, stained dress and replaced it with one of his black T-shirts. It was so large and long that it covered more than that dress ever had, falling to just above my knees. The neckline was so wide that it kept falling off and revealing one of my shoulders, but instead of struggling with it, I left it like that.

When I exited the bathroom, I was met with three masculine stares. The possessiveness in Blake's gaze was unmistakable as he scanned me up and down. It made me remember that I was wearing *his* shirt. I knew that for a fact because it smelled like him.

The other two were more difficult to read. I could tell that Kevin had more questions. No doubt Blake had been out here telling them all about my scars. I should have felt my ears burning.

I wrapped my arms around my waist, waiting for one of them to speak, to give me chores to do, to ask questions, whatever. This silence was weighing me down.

Kevin crooked a finger and said, "Come here."

I shot a hesitant glance at Blake before complying. Kevin didn't like having to repeat himself, so I approached him, uncertainty warring in my gut.

He shocked the hell out of me when he squatted and took one of my knees in his hand. His thumb caressed the visible bruises.

"I don't understand. You're a wolf shifter, are you not?" he asked, his eyes locked with mine.

I nodded. "Yes, I am."

"These should have healed by now." His brow furrowed. "Why haven't they healed?"

At least he hadn't phrased his question as, *What's wrong with you?*

The truth was always the best course with these three—at least so far.

"I'm a weak wolf. That's why my pack rejected me, and why I don't heal right." I hated saying it out loud. Hated telling them something that they could use to hurt me. Too many of Arik's business associates thought it was fun—the wolf-girl who would scar, and they got creative with what they inflicted on me.

"Let me see your palms," Kevin said.

Chewing the inside of my cheek, I hesitated. My goal had been to hide all of this from them.

Kevin patiently held out his huge hands. I placed mine in his, his heat warming my skin, and opened my palms. The skin was rough and red, marked by blisters. It looked worse than it felt.

Nathaniel growled, and I shot him a startled glance. But his gaze wasn't on me, it was boring into the side of Blake's head. Suddenly, the air thickened with danger. I didn't understand what was going on. Surely Nathaniel wasn't *upset* about my wounded hands. That was all part of my punishment, which I took without complaint. Besides, how were they to know that I couldn't heal right away like all other shifters?

"Take it outside," Kevin ordered them, but his attention remained on me.

They lumbered out the door. The porch creaked beneath their weight, then I heard the splintering sound of bones shifting into new forms, followed by monstrous roars.

"What just happened?" I asked. "What's wrong?"

Kevin stood up and towered over me. "Nothing. They have some pent-up anger to take out on each other. They'll be fine."

Snarls sounded through the cabin windows and I knew they were fighting each other. But why? Their brutal grunts and roars made me cringe. I frowned with concern.

Kevin caught my chin. "Don't worry about it. Let's get you patched up."

I stared up at him, confused. "Why?"

A lead weight plummeted in my stomach. Did he want to heal me so that he could do something worse later? It wouldn't be the first time someone had done that to me.

Echoes of voices surfaced in my brain. *Hold her down. Don't worry, he's going to heal you and make it all better. Hold her down. This is how I make her scream.*

I felt the blood drain from my face.

"Gem, I don't know what you're thinking, but no one is going to hurt you." He caressed my cheek. "That includes us, sweetheart."

Sweetheart? Was I losing my mind?

"But you're supposed to be punishing me for what I did."

He sighed. "Things have changed." He released my chin, but didn't step away.

"What things?" Wariness colored my words.

Kevin leaned down until his lips were mere inches from mine. My breath caught in my lungs.

"Can't you feel it?" he asked.

"Feel what?" My heart pounded in my chest like it wanted to escape. His leather and cognac scent made my head spin slightly, and my eyelashes fluttered.

"Never mind." With a slight frown, he pulled away. "From now on, you're under our protection."

It took a moment for my head to clear. "I'm under your protection." I repeated him, trying to make sense of his words. "You mean for the next three months?"

He paused, his hazel eyes shimmering with his inner bear. "Yes. For the next three months."

"What changed?" I pressed the issue. Their one-eighty attitude shift was making me dizzy. One second, I'm theirs to punish, and the next, they want to protect me?

Kevin sighed again. "Nothing. You are still bound by our agreement. You will do anything and everything we ask of you, without limitation or complaint. Now sit down so I can tend to your injuries."

I did as I was told. Not going to lie, I was completely baffled by them. Why were both Blake and Kevin suddenly pretending to care? Why were Nathaniel and Blake outside right now fighting each other?

Why did I feel like they were all keeping a monumental secret?

This six-foot-four bear of a man kneeled beside me, rubbing balm first on my bruised knees, and then on my ruined palms. His touch was surprisingly gentle for such a rugged giant. If I didn't know any better, I'd think I was dreaming. This turn of events was giving me a headache.

What had changed? Blake had seen my scars, I'd confessed my greatest weakness and shame as a shifter, and told them the truth about the key points of my past.

"I don't want your pity," I said. That was the only logical explanation as to why they were treating me differently. They took pity on the poor weak wolf-girl with an abusive past—and probably future—and couldn't stomach adding to my misery.

I was beginning to sound like a pessimist. Or was I actually a realist?

One thing I knew for sure, pity never helped anyone. It was one of those emotions that made people feel better about themselves, and at its worst, a justification for their actions.

Arik had taken pity on me in that alley. From that day on, he'd said I owed him for what he did for me. No matter how much I did for him, no matter the price I paid, I was never released from that debt. Anything I did was never enough.

Kevin's warm brown eyes flicked to my face. "*Pity* is the one thing you don't have from me, sweetheart."

What kind of cryptic answer was that?

"Blake told me about your scars," he said, focusing on wrapping my hands in long strips of cloth. "Was it Arik who did that to you?"

I clenched my teeth, hating talking about this subject. "It's in the past. Does it matter?"

His sharp gaze caught mine. "Yes, it matters." Danger hovered around him in thick clouds, and I shrunk back in the chair. "Who hurt you?" he demanded.

I shook my head. "It doesn't matter. I don't want to talk about it."

"Who. Hurt. You?" His tone insisted that I answer him. "You know I don't like repeating myself." Having finished with my hands, he stood, gripped the arms of the chair, and leaned in so we were face-to-face.

I had to tilt my head way back to meet his eyes as he stared down at me, waiting for my answer. He was all brutal intimidation that commanded every ounce of my attention. My vision was filled with his handsome features, his scent consumed my senses, and his body heat settled deep beneath my skin.

Yet instead of feeling frightened, I felt empowered. I could face him head-on.

I straightened my spine. The action was a relatively small one, but in that moment, something clicked in me, the flip of a switch. Or maybe more of a thing pushed too far, and it finally snapped. Rage coursed through my veins and flushed my skin. My heart pounded with fury.

"No," I said. "I don't want to talk about it." I stretched up enough to be right in his face. "I'm so tired of doing what I'm told. Of-of men like you bossing me around. No matter what I do, or sacrifice, it's never enough. All you do is take, take, take, and I've had enough!

"I know coming in here and eating your food was wrong, but I was cold and hungry and left to die in these woods. I'm not making excuses. If you want to punish me, fine. But I will not owe you for patching me up, or throwing me scraps of food, or for anything else. When our agreement is over, I'm leaving. I'm never coming back. So do your worst, because I've sure as shit survived more than you could ever throw at me." I glared up at him. Pride, at having for once stood up for myself, glowed in my chest.

While I spoke, Kevin's eyes turned from hazel to deep, dark pools of liquid heat. A pause followed my controlled outburst. He searched my features, then something unreadable flickered in his gaze.

"Noted." Kevin closed the distance between us and pressed his lips against mine. I froze, stunned, the kiss at odds with my anger and his cool tone.

He ran the tip of his tongue across my bottom lip and my body sparked to life. Heat shot straight between my thighs, my eyelids closed, and a soft moan escaped my throat. My bandaged hands moved of their own accord, my fingers sinking into his soft brown-and-gray hair. Finally, I parted my lips and let him in.

As if that was what he'd been waiting for, he plundered my mouth with his tongue. He tasted of warmth and expensive whiskey. My nipples peaked, aching for his touch. A dizzying need to have his cock filling me up made me tremble. I'd never desired a man so much before in my life.

Sex up to this point had been a necessity, survival, submission. I was never asked if I wanted it or not. Desire was not part of the equation. It was an exchange.

But with Kevin, I wanted him. Every fiber of my being craved him.

I clenched my thighs together, trying to alleviate my throbbing clit. The movement only made it worse. Kevin had yet to touch my body, and I was so close to some... unexplainable precipice.

He broke our kiss to gently bite my lower lip. "Do you feel it now?"

"I-I want... I need..." I whimpered, unsure of how to complete my sentence. Instinctively, I knew I was asking for something, but I didn't know what.

"I know what you need, sweetheart. Come here." Kevin lifted me from the chair and placed my butt on the kitchen countertop. He stood in front of me and I wrapped my legs around his hips.

This time his kiss was soft, unhurried. One of his

enormous hands settled on my waist while the other rested on my thigh. His thumb drew small circles on my blazing flesh as he inched under the hem of the T-shirt and closer to my core.

When he reached it, he found me hot and wet for him. At his very first touch, I moaned and spread my thighs wider. His thumb dipped into my wet pussy, then teased my clit, and I gasped as pleasure overtook me.

Kevin trailed kisses over my jaw and down my neck. I let my head fall back. Never in my life had I experienced anything like this. Every nerve ending was on fire, but it didn't hurt. I reveled in the intensity of the inferno. Pressure built low in my stomach and my breathing became ragged. I was so close to... something.

That *something* hit me like a freight train a moment later. My entire body went taut as wave after wave of pure ecstasy crashed over me. My fingers dug into Kevin's shoulders, my forehead buried in his chest, as I cried out again and again.

Every ounce of energy left me and my muscles turned to goo. For the first time in forever, my mind was completely blank, devoid of memory or thought. I simply *was*, as if frozen in time and space.

Kevin planted a kiss on my forehead. "Are you all right?"

"I think so." I summoned up enough strength to shyly meet his gaze. "What *was* that?"

His warm brown eyes clouded with confusion. "What was...?" Clarity dawned. "You've never had an orgasm before?" His tone was somewhere between surprise and horror.

My cheeks blazed. I thought I'd had at least one or two before, but I guessed... not. "Um, no." I ducked my head.

Kevin caught my chin, making me look up at him again. His eyes darkened with anger. "I'm going to make this right for you, Gem. That's a promise."

I didn't know exactly what he meant by those words, but they rang with sincerity.

After my very first orgasm, Kevin had fed me breakfast. Then he sat me in his rocking chair to relax in front of the fireplace. He was quiet and broody for the rest of the day, keeping to himself and seeming deep in thought. I took the opportunity to snooze. I was exhausted from *everything*.

Blake and Nathaniel returned in the early evening. Both of them were streaked with blood, and my pulse stuttered at the sight of them. I'd seen plenty of nude shifters in my life, but hot damn, those two entering the cabin stole the breath right out of my lungs.

Blake's tattoos actually did cover nearly every inch of his body. His black hair rested on his shoulders, framing his gorgeous face.

Nathaniel was all golden blond, his hair tousled and would have been sexy except for the coldness of his icy-green eyes. They warned off anyone who dared to look for too long. When he caught my assessing glance, his sharpened, and I quickly averted my gaze.

Without a word, naked, they marched upstairs.

"Excuse me," Kevin said. Peeling himself out of the chair beside me, he lumbered up the stairs after them.

Quiet settled over the cabin. That, and the warmth of the blazing fire lulled me back to sleep.

"This is how you make her scream." Arik's voice cut through the haze of pain. He tapped the ash from his cigar, then puffed on it until it flared crimson. Holding me down, he seared my skin and I did. I screamed. Tears streamed down my face.

The men around us laughed.

Arik continued, "She was a virgin when I found her last year. Pathetic little creature. I popped that cherry, but if we close this deal tonight, you can keep her until dawn. Believe me, her pussy is still tight and fresh. She won't disappoint."

Four pairs of lustful eyes turned on me, devouring my nearly naked body and making my skin crawl.

Arik whispered in my ear, "Be a good girl and scream for them, otherwise they'll hurt you beyond repair. And remember, you owe me this. I've fed you, clothed you, given you pretty things, too. Haven't I? What do you say to me?"

"Th-thank you."

He barked a laugh. "See, she's so polite too."

They spoke, smoking and drinking, for another few minutes before they shook hands with Arik. My heart thumped so rapidly, I thought I'd die. This was it. Their deal was done, and I was part of the agreement.

Only until dawn.

I thought Arik would leave right away, but he didn't. Instead, he held me down while the four men put their cigars out on my stomach. Their eyes lit with satisfaction as I screamed and begged for them to stop.

One of them tore my panties off and—

"Gem! Sweetheart, wake up." The deep, smooth voice brought me out of the nightmare. My throat felt sore, like I'd been screaming in my sleep. I blinked up at him.

We were on the floor, Kevin holding me to his chest, smoothing my hair away from my face. Blake and Nathaniel hovered nearby, both of them clean and dressed in jeans and T-shirts.

How long had I been asleep?

"You okay, princess?" Blake moved closer and squatted beside us. He brushed a stray strand of hair from my sweaty forehead. "You had a nightmare that wouldn't let you go."

I swallowed hard, remembering my dream—or rather, reliving my past while I slept. Digging up my past over these last few days was churning up all kinds of things I'd rather forget, including, and especially, *that* night. A tremor tore through me, and Kevin held me closer.

Suddenly, I felt suffocated. Thick panic and fear oozed from my pores. I had to get away. I needed air.

I scrambled out of Kevin's hold and kept going until my back smacked against the cabin door. A pair of brown, blue, and green eyes all watched me with curiosity and concern. They could smell my fear. I knew they could.

I'd grown so numb to the horrors of my existence that I rarely felt anything other than apathy. Except right now, I was feeling everything, too much, and some of these feelings were new to me.

I was fine when the bears staring at me had promised punishment and pain. That, I was familiar with enough to block out. But this gentle, caring approach was fucking with my head. It was tearing past my protective walls and exposing my vulnerabilities. Worst of all, it was giving me hope.

Hope was a dangerous emotion. One that could destroy me if I wasn't careful.

Kevin approached like I was a frightened animal ready to bolt, while Blake and Nathaniel held back, giving me space.

My heart pounded against my ribs with bruising force.

"You're okay, sweetheart. I've got you," he said, his hand outstretched. His fingertips caressed my cheek. "You're safe now. Nothing and no one will hurt you."

I shouldn't believe him, but his words floated past my barriers and anchored themselves deep in my heart. I wanted to believe him. I *wanted* to be safe. The most this world ever offered me was the illusion of safety.

"Come here," Kevin said so softly that all my resistance crumbled. I stepped into his embrace. Letting his warmth, scent, and innate danger cloak me, I melted into him. He felt like a shield against the world, against my past. My own personal shield to keep away the demons.

9
GEM

Every time I tried to open my eyes, to pull myself out of sleep, the softness of the silky pillow against my cheek, and the warmth of the blankets dragged me back under. Cognac and leather, with a hint of woodsmoke, teased my nose. The scent was so delicious, I wanted to lick it.

I tried to roll over but something heavy rested across my stomach and pinned me in place. When I continued to wiggle, that weight scooped me up and held me against a wall of muscle. Being cuddled, encased in heat and strength, was an odd but amazing sensation.

Wait, cuddled?

My eyes popped open. I lay in a darkened room, the dawn light peeking through the curtains. The soft glow illuminated the sleeping man at my back. His soft snores ruffled my hair.

I stilled, assessing the situation. How had I ended up here in Kevin's room last night? I racked my brain, and slowly, memories surfaced of me having a freaking panic attack and Kevin's comforting, soft baritone smoothing it all away. *Safe. Protected. Hope.* Then he'd taken me to his bed to sleep. Just to sleep.

This was all new territory for me and I was having difficulty wrapping my brain around it. I was their captive for ninety days, yet... *everything* had shifted. I felt it deep within myself, even though I couldn't identify what it was specifically.

In the quiet of the morning, I let my thoughts and feelings wander. Normally, I'd panic about being held this closely and tightly by an enormous man in his bed, but that tightening in my chest and thundering heartbeat never came. Instead, it felt *good*. I wanted nothing more than to snuggle into his heat, his large body a barrier against the outside world, and stay there forever.

"Morning, sweetheart," he gruffly rumbled.

Even the timbre of his voice seemed to wrap me in a protective cocoon.

"Good morning." I squirmed against him to get as close as possible. That was when I felt the rigidness of his cock against my ass. He groaned, and I froze.

It was morning and he was hard. Heat pooled between my legs, taking me by surprise as I realized that I *wanted* to feel him inside of me.

With another soft groan, he peeled himself away and turned to lie on his back. I followed his movements, turning all the way over, and tentatively rested my hand on his bare chest. His warm hazel eyes searched my face. I trailed my palm along his skin, and his chest rose and fell more rapidly. His lips parted when I reached his stomach.

Before I could venture lower, he caught my wrist. "What are you doing?"

"Repaying you for yesterday." I wanted to give him the same pleasure he'd given me. That orgasm had been out of this world. I wondered if I could give him that kind of pleasure.

His features shuttered. "You don't owe me anything." He released my hand and climbed out of bed, quickly getting dressed. "It's time for breakfast."

The sexual tension between us snapped and dissipated, leaving a chill over the room.

I frowned at him. What had I done wrong?

For the first time, I joined them at the table for breakfast. Quietly nibbling on a biscuit, I sat between Kevin and Blake, directly in the line of sight of Nathaniel's glare. At this point, I was convinced he had no other facial expression.

Blake kept eyeing Kevin and me like he was trying to figure out what was going on between us. So far, he hadn't asked about Kevin taking me to his bed last night. I was still curious to why Blake and Nathaniel had fought, but right now my attention was solely consumed by Kevin.

Tension still radiated from him. He was upset, and I was trying to sort out why. I revisited what I'd said to him this morning, coming to the conclusion that it was my wording that had offended him.

I hadn't meant *repay* as in I was only doing it because I felt I owed him, and felt obligated to pleasure him. But I had a feeling that was how he had taken it.

I was slightly shocked to realize that I could actually hurt his feelings. I hadn't meant to hurt him, but that was what happened. Now I needed to figure out how to make it right, how to tell him that I wanted him out of desire, and not as a transaction. I wasn't sure what was brewing between us but it felt like it could be significant.

Not paying attention, I reached for the honey jar at the same time as Nathaniel. My fingers brushed over his and a shot of electricity zipped up my arm. I gave a startled yelp, and he dropped the ceramic jar as if it had burned him. It landed with a loud thud on the table.

Kevin and Blake spared us curious glances, but nobody said a word. The tension was so thick all around that I could cut it with a knife.

I shook off the strange electrical sensation as best I could. It had probably been a bit of static in the air. What other explanation was there?

After a beat, Blake picked up the honey jar and set it beside me. The act of kindness took me by surprise. Nathaniel's scowl deepened, but that didn't deter me from shyly smiling at Blake and slathering my biscuit with honey.

Blake finally broke the strained silence. "I was out before dawn this morning," he said to Kevin. "No sign of that wolf pack. I think they've moved on for good."

The older bear nodded. "That may be the case. Even so, we continue with our patrol schedule. I don't want us to be taken by surprise again." Kevin took a sip of coffee.

"Why do they keep coming back?" I asked. It wasn't normal for wolves to antagonize bears. They were both highly territorial shifters and preferred to keep their distance from others.

"From what I can tell," Kevin said. "They're a migrant outcast pack looking for a new home. Their willingness to take on three bears to steal territory shows how desperate they are. As for why here? I don't know."

"That is strange," I said.

Kevin gazed down at me, assessing. Even though we barely knew each other, I hated this small distance that had grown between us and took away the warmth. Emboldened, I let my palm rest on his thigh. His muscles tensed, but he didn't pull away or say anything about the touch, so I kept my hand there through the remainder of breakfast.

I helped Blake clean up, washing the dishes, and wiping down the table. His T-shirt was all I had to wear, and I caught him eyeing me from time to time with overt possessiveness. His gaze sent shivers of awareness across my skin. At the same time, guilt crawled into my stomach and made me queasy. I was wearing Blake's shirt but sleeping in Kevin's bed. I'd let Kevin kiss and touch me yesterday, too.

What the fuck was I doing?

While I was drying the plates, Blake came up behind

me and looped an arm around my waist. I stiffened. My stomach swooped with anxiety and anticipation.

He leaned down and spoke into my ear, "I know what happened on this countertop yesterday. Mm, your scent still lingers, and it's making my mouth water."

My lips parted in shock.

He continued, "As much as I love seeing you in my clothes, I think it's time you wore something less... distracting." He growled that last word and my thighs clenched. These men were wreaking havoc on my body.

I said the first thing that came to mind. "I-I don't have anything else to wear."

"We'll have to fix that." Kevin strode to us, his gaze assessing, and he turned me to face him. Blake remained at my back, effectively sandwiching me between their two massive forms. Kevin tipped my chin up. "We'll go to town today and get you everything you need."

My head swam from their proximity, but I managed a simple, "Okay."

Kevin ducked down and placed a soft kiss on my lips. Behind me, Blake's hold on my waist tightened, and heat shot straight between my legs.

Traitorous body. I wasn't anywhere near ready to warm up to this new side of Blake. Blake the Asshole was all too fresh in my memory.

"Come on." Kevin took my hand in his and tugged me out of Blake's arms. "There's a resort town about an hour's run from here. We'll find everything we need there."

I glanced over my shoulder to find narrowed blue

eyes staring after us. What did he think? He could do a one-eighty on me and suddenly I'd jump into bed with him? Letting me wear his clothes, handing me the honey jar, and whispering filthy words in my ear were not going to erase how much I could tell he enjoyed punishing me.

The chores I could handle. It was being woken up, drenched in ice water, his pettiness, and the way he watched me like I was his next meal that I didn't particularly care for.

I clung tighter to Kevin's hand. He led us out the door and the other two followed.

Outside, standing in the frozen woodland, Blake and Nathaniel undressed and shifted. Their black and honey-blond bear forms were enormous. On instinct, I took a step away from them.

Kevin caught me around the waist. "I need you not to be afraid, sweetheart. As bears, we can make the journey faster." He placed the lightest of kisses on my forehead. "I want you to ride on my back. Can you do that for me?"

"I..." The thought of a wolf shifter riding on a bear's back was laughable. But my only choices seemed to be, do as he asked, shift, or walk beside them on bare feet. Walking, I would significantly slow them down.

Shifting was out of the question.

So that left... I nodded. "I can do that."

"Good girl. Now put this satchel across your shoulder. Our clothes and other things are in there, so don't lose that. Once I've shifted, I want you to climb up on my back, and hold tight around my neck. All right?"

"Okay."

He stripped down and shifted forms. His fur was a rich brown that matched his eyes. I grasped a handful of it and pulled myself up until I was straddling his back, then looped my arms around his neck.

Kevin took off at a run and I firmed up my hold. Soon they were racing through the trees, the wind whipping my hair back, and a lightness ballooning in my stomach. I felt free, and alive.

I felt like I was flying. The feeling of weightlessness was amazing, exhilarating. For the first time in years, a genuine smile spread my lips wide.

10
NATHANIEL

Morons. I genuinely cared about and loved my bear brothers, but sometimes they were both fucking dense as could be. Like now, for example. While Gem was in the dressing room, Blake was choosing lacy underwear and bra sets for her, while Kevin had gone off to find her a smoothie after she'd briefly mentioned having one in the past and liking it.

Doting on her was completely understandable. The problem was they didn't understand why they had such urges. It wasn't because they were lonely, nor was it because she was pretty, vulnerable, and fucking perfect. Neither pity nor remorse factored into it either.

She's our mate, you fucking idiots. I'd known it from the first whiff of her scent.

At our first encounter, with Blake's rough hold on her, and Kevin's anger unleashed at the she-wolf he'd found sleeping in his bed, I'd been on the verge of stepping in. But I hadn't. Why? Because the last thing I wanted was a mate. Especially one as naïve and damaged as Gem.

Damage, I understood all too well. After hearing her story the other night, it confirmed my suspicions that if I claimed her, I'd completely ruin her. She was too sweet, innocent, and naïve for a man like me.

Were the fates trying to punish us both?

The past week had been torture, as Blake made her miserable with his punishments. Though the recent turn of events with his and Kevin's hands and eyes all over her body was excruciating in a totally different way. I refused to touch her. But watching them touch her drove home how much I *wanted* that contact. My bear yearned for it and there was only so long I could deny him. We should have sent her away when there was still a chance for her to run.

Too late now.

"I don't think I need this." Gem stepped out from the fitting room, wearing a long blue dress that made her skin glow and her eyes sparkle. The silk hugged every one of her curves.

Fuck, she was gorgeous. Her golden hair, with hints of red, flowed down her back. I wanted to wrap her locks around my fist like Blake had done that first day. I'd have her gaze up at me with those wide blue eyes full of fear. Her whimpers and moans would fill my ears as I fucked her hard.

I blinked, snapping myself out of my deranged fantasy. *That* was why I stayed away from her. After a lifetime of torturing people for pay, something inside me was broken, and I got off on inflicting pain.

Fate was a cruel bitch to put this damaged, tempting little wolf-girl in my path. I'd only give her more pain, more trauma, and more scars. Worse, it would make me fucking *happy.*

It would also drive a wedge between me and my chosen brothers. They would try to protect her from me, and either both of them or I would end up dead.

Gem spun in the dress. "This is hardly practical for gathering firewood."

"It's for when we go out to a club or something," Blake said. "You should get it."

Her delicate brow pinched. "But you live in the middle of the woods. There are no clubs around."

"Doesn't mean we can't go out on the town from time to time." Blake's lazy gaze swept over her and I narrowed my eyes at all the filthy thoughts I knew were going on in his head. Similar ones were playing in my own.

"You really think we're going to go out during the next couple of months?" She sounded both uncertain and hopeful and so fucking adorable.

"I think we can make that happen." Blake shot her a wink, and she blushed.

My inner bear snarled, both from her attention on Blake and from the thought of her leaving us. Kevin and Blake might be under the impression she was only our temporary guest, but I knew that she wasn't going anywhere. Ever. She was mine.

Mine. Mine. Mine.

It didn't matter that I didn't deserve her. Or that I might break her. Every moment would be the sweetest indulgence.

Kevin returned, handing her a strawberry banana smoothie like it was a prize. He convinced her to keep the dress, then his eye caught mine. As if he could read the wicked thoughts going through my mind, his gaze darkened with warning.

I inwardly scoffed. He and Blake were acting like mighty protectors now, but neither of them could fool themselves forever. They might not be as fucked up as I was, but they certainly weren't *good* either. Gem would find that out for herself at some point.

In the meantime, I amused myself by keeping my trap shut and watching this all unfold. Even she didn't realize she was fated to us. I wasn't sure why that hadn't dawned on her awareness yet, but it hadn't.

Blake piled a myriad of silk and lace underwear in her arms, as her cheeks glowed a brighter pink, and he turned her toward the dressing room. I rolled my eyes at him. Could he be any more obvious?

Kevin strolled up beside me. "I know that look, Nathaniel. Just so we're clear, she will never be one of your playthings. In fact, step outside with me."

I followed him out of the shop. A brisk wind swept through the small plaza as a cold winter sun blazed down on us. Few other shoppers were out at this time of day. Most of the tourists were either on the slopes or in the spas.

Kevin's bear flashed in his eyes. "She's my mate. You won't lay a hand on her."

I couldn't help it, I laughed. Genuinely laughed out loud. The sound was foreign even to my ears.

His eyes narrowed. "What's so damn funny?"

"Everything." I chuckled, wiping at my tearing eyes. "She's fated to *all* of us, boss. You, me, and Blake."

His brows lifted to his hairline. I could see the wheels churning in his mind as he processed through my statement. He pinned me with a deadly stare.

"You've known since that first night," he growled.

Even though it wasn't a question, I nodded and shoved my hands into my jean's pockets, shoulders hunched.

"I had a feeling that she and Blake might be... But you?" Kevin surveyed me like I was a bug under a microscope. "Fate wouldn't be so cruel to either of you."

"Oh yes she would. Fate's a bitch, boss." I leaned casually against a pillar, looking out at the square. "You know it's only a matter of time before I claim her, and there's nothing you can do about it."

He growled low, threatening. "Gem doesn't seem to know yet. Why?"

I shook my head. "She doesn't. Not yet. I'm not sure why." I glanced at him. "Are you going to try to stop me from making her mine?"

A long stretch of tense silence hovered between us. Finally, he said, "No. Fate put her in your path for a reason. Maybe Gem is different. Maybe you'll be different with her."

I very much doubted that. But at least, when the time came, Kevin wouldn't stand in my way. Blake, on the other hand, he was unpredictable and hot-headed.

Who knew what the fuck he'd do. My lips twisted in a grimace.

Blake and Gem exited the store, him carrying three huge shopping bags. She was dressed in a pair of jeans, a blouse, and a wool coat. Even fully clothed, she looked good enough to eat.

I tagged along as we spent the day at several more boutiques and other stores. Kevin and Blake lavished her with an entire wardrobe, female necessities, and an array of accessories that filled every single pack we'd brought.

The subtext was quite clear—they were keeping her forever. Good.

11

GEM

After the long run home, we ate a simple but delicious dinner around the table. Having my own clothes, and other necessities covered, made me feel like my own person again. However, the satisfaction of it was tainted by the fact that *they* had bought everything for me. Just like with Arik, I was indebted to them.

I couldn't keep living like this. I needed to somehow break this cycle.

Regret twisted in my stomach as I remembered just how much they'd bought—clothes, shoes, two coats, a purse, and so much more. It was too much. I should have insisted on a couple of outfits and that would have been fine. Even then, I would still owe them, so did it really make a difference?

A debt was a debt.

Once we were finished with dinner, Kevin said, "Come with me." He took my hand in his and stood.

"But I should help clean up." I gestured to the table with my free hand.

"Leave it." He towed me up the stairs. All the while, I felt Blake's gaze boring into my back. I glanced over my shoulder to confirm it. His eyes flashed with dark possessiveness and my heart lurched.

Upstairs, Kevin took me to his room and gently closed the door. "What's eating away at you?" he asked.

My lips parted in surprise. How could he tell something was bothering me? Was I that transparent?

"Nothing," I lied. *Wrong move.*

Kevin closed the distance between us and cupped my jaw with his massive hands. "Tell me the truth. You seemed happy today in town. What changed when we returned home?"

I had a feeling he wouldn't release me until I told him, so I gave in. "I don't like being indebted to anyone. You bought me too many nice things today and I feel bad about it because I have no way of paying you back."

His eyes softened. He brushed his thumb across my lower lip. "Even though we bought you many things today, you owe us absolutely nothing." He sighed at my silent stare that called *bullshit*. "Okay, maybe we didn't act out of the kindness of our hearts. At least not exactly. But this situation is unique."

My heartbeat quickened as apprehension sent a chill through me. I was right. No one ever did anything kind for another person for no reason. There was always a catch.

"Gem, sweetheart, I need to tell you something so you'll understand. Though I think it may be better to show you instead." He stepped closer, his heat seeping beneath my skin. "Fate has brought us together. I'm not entirely sure why, or why now, but I couldn't live with myself if I didn't give you a choice. Lady Fate may have spoken, but this last choice is yours to make."

I frowned up at him, unsure of what the hell he was talking about, or where he was going with this topic. "What choice do I have to make now?"

Fate *had* brought us together. I'd been ditched in their woods and left with no other option but to enter their home uninvited, invading their privacy and facing their wrath.

"You need to decide whether to stay or go. Tonight. Though I can't promise I won't hunt you down if you decide to leave." He pressed my back against the wall. "What I can tell you is that we are hard men. I was head of a large crime syndicate's security before I retired here. I've done unthinkable things. Wicked things." His breath warmed my face. "I want to do wicked things to you, sweetheart."

I expected panic to cloud my mind, but in its place came my pounding pulse as desire pooled low in my stomach. My sensitive nipples poked against the lace of my bra. If he was trying to warn me away, he was doing a horrible job of it. I felt deep in my heart that Kevin would never hurt me. He was nothing like Arik.

I licked my lips. "What kind of wicked things would you do to me?"

"Very wicked things." His eyes darkened to pools of obsidian. "If you stay, I will claim you as my own. I will mark you for the world to see. Fate demands it. I want it with every fiber of my being."

I sucked in a harsh breath. Fate. He thought we were fated? My stunned brain took a moment to jumpstart, then everything clicked into place. Everything about Kevin appealed to me—his voice, his scent, his presence. I felt safe with him because my inner wolf knew that he was my match.

Was that why I'd chosen his bed to fall asleep in on my first day here?

I thought back to the bears finding me in their house. Their threats and anger had terrified me, yet at the same time, deep down, I'd felt safer in their presence than I had in a long time.

It all made sense. Kevin was my fated mate.

I reached within, trying to touch the she-wolf buried deep below the surface, but she remained quiet. Even without her confirmation, I knew the truth. I could see it now. Only one question remained. Was this what I wanted?

I spoke around the thick lump in my throat. "And if I leave?"

"You'll probably be running forever. I'll try to leave you alone, but I can't honestly make you that promise." His words sent a shiver down my spine. "The choice is yours. I need you to decide now, before it's too late. Will you stay, or will you run?"

It wasn't much of a decision. I could be his now, or he'd eventually come after me and drag me back to him. Shifters were possessive by nature and bears more so than most. Either way, I'd eventually be his.

I gave myself a moment to let that reality sink in. The thought of being his, and him being mine, sent a rush of warmth over my skin.

Strangely, I wasn't particularly bothered by his dark past. He was a dangerous man, but because of that, I felt safer in his presence instead of afraid. I trusted that he could defeat any threat that came for me, or us.

Unlike other dangerous men I'd met, Kevin wasn't also cruel. He was a protector at heart. I saw it in how he treated me every single day. No, this man—my true mate—wouldn't abuse me. I was safe with him. Safe from the world, from those who wanted to hurt me. Being his mate had a certain appeal.

I released the breath I hadn't realized I was holding in. "I want to be yours." My voice came out hushed.

"Then you will be." He crushed his lips to mine. Our tongues slid against each other, as he picked me up and laid me on his bed. Slowly, he stripped away my clothes as if he was unwrapping a gift. His rough hands and warm hazel gaze heated every inch of my skin. He explored every mound and hollow, teasing my nipples into peaks, and cupping my sex like he owned it— owned me.

That blatant display of dominance should have frightened me, but with him, it didn't. With him, I felt cherished, seen, and valued.

When my chest rose, quick and shallow, he stood and began to undress. His gaze never left my body. Mine roamed his as he revealed heavy muscles, and thick, corded limbs. He was huge in every way. My thighs grew wetter at the sight of such powerful masculinity.

Kevin climbed onto the bed, spreading my legs wide with his knees. He dipped his fingers into my pussy and hummed with approval.

"You're so wet for me," he groaned. "That's a good girl." His words jolted pleasure straight to my cunt.

I thought he was going to push his erection into me, but instead, he surprised me by stroking my pussy while flicking the tip of his tongue over my nipples. He tasted my body, teasing me until I was writhing beneath him.

"Please," I gasped when he sucked my nipple into his wicked mouth again. This was excruciating torture, and I needed a release, soon. Especially now that I knew what an orgasm felt like.

Without answering me, he replaced his fingers with his cock. I was so wet that he easily slid in with one powerful thrust. I turned my head to the side and closed my eyes.

Kevin gently nudged my chin, making me face him. "Eyes open. I want to see all of you, every thought and feeling as I make you come on my dick."

My eyes widened at his filthy words. I did as I was told, and he started moving his hips. Soon, I was lost in the sensations floating through my body, the tension coiling in my stomach, and the feel of his calloused hands on my smooth skin. My eyelids slid closed on a moan.

"Eyes on me," he said in a rough voice.

My gaze locked with his.

"Good girl." He picked up his pace, his thumb circled my clit, and I could tell I wasn't going to last much longer. Struggling to keep my eyes open, pleasure shot through me and I clenched around his hard length.

"*Fuck*," he swore, adjusting his angle and hitting a spot inside that immediately sent another orgasm crashing over me. This time, his teeth bit into the flesh above my collarbone, and I came again.

Instinct drove me to bite down on his shoulder, marking him as mine. We both shuddered. His release pulsed deep in my cunt. He lowered his forehead and rested it on mine.

A tremble shook my body. That had been the most intimate sex I'd ever had, and by far the best. I realized there was a difference between being used as a fuck toy and having sex with another person as their equal. I'd never experienced the latter until now.

The aftermath shook my world. This was it. We'd marked each other as our mates. Our essences mingled, and we were tied together for the rest of our lives. Panic bubbled up at my seemingly rash decision. I whimpered.

"Shh," he murmured. "I've got you, sweetheart." He placed a gentle kiss on my lips.

Rolling to the side, he wrapped me in his embrace, pulling me to his chest. A bit awkwardly, I snuggled into him. His woodsy, masculine scent calmed my racing heart.

My breathing evened out and my eyelids drooped. Everything about this felt right, like I'd returned to a home I hadn't realized I'd been missing. Calm settled in my chest.

"Your ours now, and you will never want for

anything. I promise. You have our protection. What is ours is now yours. Forever."

Ours?

I opened my mouth to question his word choice, but sleep dragged me under before I could make a single utterance.

The snow was little more than slush this morning. An overcast sky diffused the sun's rays, casting an even glow through the forest clearing. I carried a basket half full of winter herbs I'd gathered not far from the cabin.

All three bears were already out patrolling their territory when I woke this morning. Kevin had told me to sleep as long as I liked, and they'd be back later. I'd slept in until nearly noon, fixed myself a simple breakfast, then decided to step outside for some much-needed fresh air.

As long as I stuck close to the cabin, I figured it was safe enough for me to go for a short walk. The crisp air would help clear my head. Fates knew I needed it after last night's claiming. A flash of heat swept straight to my pussy at the memory.

Last night had changed everything. For the first time in my life, I felt like I belonged, was cherished and wanted. I'd found my fated mate which was something I thought would never happen. It was a blessing among shifters. A blessing that was bestowed upon the worthy.

Confusion knit my brow. Had Fate found me worthy? Had she made a mistake?

I bent down and plucked a spear-shaped leaf from a plant growing beside a small stream. Rubbing it between my fingers, I released its oils and took a whiff, confirming it was mint.

As I gathered the herb, my mind wandered from Kevin to Blake. His possessive stare said he wanted me for himself. A flush briefly warmed my skin. How was he going to react to Kevin claiming me instead? And why, since I found my fated one, was I thinking about another man? Blake should have no effect me, and yet... I couldn't shake the memory of his large hands exploring my scars with such tenderness, and his anger on my behalf. My heart clenched.

Protective Blake was growing on me now that I hadn't seen Asshole Blake in a while.

The birds enjoying a break in the cloud cover suddenly fell silent. Was there a predator nearby? My first thought was that one of the guys had returned early, but as I stood, the hairs on the back of my neck bristled.

I spun around, searching the denser shadows beneath the trees. Someone was there, watching me, I could feel it.

Slowly, I backed away in the direction I'd come, toward the cabin. A voice in my head screamed for me to run and get inside to safety. But running away only encouraged a predator to give chase.

A twig snapped. A menacing growl vibrated through the woods. In front of me, glowing golden eyes shone from the shadows. *Wolf shifters.* Had Arik returned for me? Or was this the pack that plagued the bears' land?

My own inner wolf should have scented them, should have sensed their presence long before my human senses picked up on them. But as usual, she remained quiet.

I was on my own.

I did the only thing I could, I turned and sped through the forest, desperate to make it back to the cabin in one piece. Sure enough, the wolves were in hot pursuit.

Panic clawed its way up my throat, but I didn't have enough air in my lungs to scream. At some point, I dropped my basket in order to fully focus on running as fast as my short legs would go.

A glance over my shoulder showed five wolves in pursuit. I pumped my arms and legs faster, but the slushy ground was hindering my escape. The wolves were quicker than me and closing in fast.

Desperately, I weaved through the stands of trees that separated me from the clearing where the cabin stood. I spotted the faint white smoke floating skyward from the stone chimney. Another minute and I would be to safety.

Up ahead, a pale brown wolf with a scar across its eye blocked my path. I dodged, altering course toward the woodshed.

I wasn't fast enough. The scarred wolf leaped into the air and tackled me to the ground. I landed hard on the wet, icy forest floor, the air leaving my lungs in a whoosh. Above me, the wolf snapped and snarled, and I lifted my arms to shield my face. His teeth sank into my forearm and I howled in pain. I brought my legs up to try to dislodge him, managing a kick to his stomach, which rewarded me with a grunt before he renewed his attack.

Another wolf caught my foot in its mouth and tugged. Pain blossomed in my ankle. Two more wolves joined in and I knew this was the end for me. They were going to literally tear me to pieces. Any humanity they'd once had was long gone.

I couldn't die like this. After everything that I'd survived, after finally finding my place in the world with my mate, I couldn't die because of a pack of feral wolves.

A flame lit in my abdomen. It was only a spark at first, but soon grew into an inferno.

A growl burst from my throat, and I continued to fight off the wolves. Heat built behind my eyes, sharpening my vision, and a presence occupied the empty space in my chest—the area reserved solely for my wolf.

I heard a devastating crack, then agony overtook my body that had nothing to do with the rabid wolves. My cry caught in my throat.

My bones crunched and twisted, reshaping themselves, as reddish-blond fur sprouted from my skin. The shifting process shut out all other sensations. It consumed me whole. My wolf was determined to break free and fight for her life—our lives.

She snarled, snapping and biting at the wolves pinning us down. Tangy blood flooded my mouth. I kicked and clawed, squirmed and growled, but they were so much larger, stronger, and my wolf was no match for the ferociousness of this pack.

The pale brown wolf latched onto the back of my neck and shook me like I was a rabbit. My head spun. I snarled at him again, unwilling to give up, even with the odds stacked against me.

He dropped me back onto the ground and four wolves descended on me at once, ripping and tearing at my fur and flesh. I released a tortured howl that echoed through the trees.

12

KEVIN

I walked the ridge in my shifted form, lumbering along a section of our territory and looking for anything amiss. The several feet of snow had melted into slippery slush this morning. Tracks would stay visible in this muck for a while before they morphed and melted away. So far, no sign of anything other than the occasional deer, raccoon, and other smaller critters.

The wind shifted directions and a multitude of scents bombarded my nose. *Wolves.* They were on our land again, somewhere lower in the valley. Motherfuckers. I took off at a gallop.

Halfway down the hillside, a terrible howl split the air. My gut twisted, and I urged my enormous limbs to move faster. My mate was in trouble. I knew with absolute certainty that it was her wolf crying out.

I reached the valley floor at the same time as Blake and Nathaniel. Our massive bear forms pounded the earth. We barreled across the clearing and into the woodlands surrounding our cabin. Fresh blood and fear colored the air. The pack of outcast wolf shifters were terrorizing a pup. Or at least that was what I first thought upon seeing the tiny wolf they were after. Then realization dawned.

No, not a pup, *Gem*.

I roared. My gaze latched onto, and never wavered from, the tiny reddish-blond she-wolf in the middle of the fray. Crimson hallowed my vision as I plowed into the wolves, slashing and biting, while being careful to avoid injuring my mate.

I managed to injure a few of them before the cowards turned tail and ran. Another roar left my throat. They could run for now, but they were all *dead*. Fucking with our territory was one thing. Attacking our mate was entirely different. Unforgivable.

Nathaniel and Blake went after them, chasing them across our border.

I shifted to my human form and kneeled beside Gem. "Sweetheart, can you hear me?"

Her wolf was so tiny that I could cradle her entire canine body in my human arms. Her eyes closed, and she shifted, unconscious. Blood, bruises, and wounds marred her naked body. Anger and fear made for an acidic mix in my stomach.

I scooped her up and nestled her against my chest. *She would be okay*, I kept telling myself during the short walk back to the cabin. She was stronger than she looked. I laid her down on the table to more closely examine the worst of her wounds.

Blake and Nathaniel barged into the cabin a few seconds later. Blake went straight to the kitchen and fetched hot water and a cloth to clean her up, while Nathaniel disappeared upstairs and returned with strips of fabric and a bottle of vodka.

The three of us went to work, patching her up as best we could. As shifters who generally healed on our own, we didn't keep a first aid kit around. We had no need for such things.

As I gently but quickly cleaned her from head to toe, rage boiled beneath my skin. Those fucking wolves had crossed the line. We would hunt them down and slaughter every last one of them for what they'd done to Gem. A quick glance at my bear brothers and I knew they were thinking the same. Blake's eyes spoke of the murderous thoughts in his head. Danger rolled off Nathaniel's tense shoulders in palpable waves.

One of us should be tracking them, but I wouldn't give the order for any one of us to leave Gem right now. She needed us, as much as we needed to see that she was going to be okay.

A couple of deeper, ugly wounds needed to be stitched. Without a word, Nathaniel went to work with a needle and thread. His stitches were so even and precise that he'd obviously done this many times before. Given his past career as a torturer, I wondered how often he'd stitched someone up to heal them rather than to prolong their life and therefore their pain.

When we finished, we washed the blood from our hands, then bundled Gem up in a soft blanket. I picked her up and sat in my chair, settling her in my lap. I wished I was still with my old Penumbra Syndicate crew, where in a situation like this, one of the Fae would heal her with magic. But here, we were all she had.

The other two took their chairs. Silently, we passed around what remained in the vodka bottle. Blake added a log to the perpetual flame, and the fire crackled to life again.

"I'm going to kill those fucking wolves for this," he spoke quietly, voicing my exact thoughts. His gaze slid to Gem sleeping in my arms. "That claiming mark is hard to miss. Care to tell us about it?"

I grunted. Like he hadn't heard us last night? I leveled my gaze on him, seeing right through his bull-shit. I decided to lay it all out for him. Nathaniel knew what she was to us, and so did I. Blake was fucking dense at times.

"She's ours." My arms instinctively tightened around her. "I claimed her last night because it was time. But she belongs to the three of us, and we belong to her."

Blake's brows shot up. "You're shitting me?"

"Do I look like I'm shitting you?" I asked in a flat tone.

He glanced over at Nathaniel, who appeared bored with our conversation. "Did you know about this?" Blake asked him.

Nathaniel nodded.

Blake huffed. "So that's why I can't keep away from her. I thought I was just getting lonely out here in the middle of nowhere with you two fuckheads for company." His brows crashed down. "She's my mate. Our mate. *Fuuuuck.*"

I rolled my eyes. Blake certainly had a way with words.

"Yes," I confirmed. "And by the small stature of her wolf, I'd say she's a runt." Knowing that she was not only petite in human form, but the smallest, most delicate wolf I'd ever seen, brought out an undeniable need to protect her. A possessive growl rumbled in my chest.

"She said her birth pack, her family, cast her out because she wasn't good enough for them," Blake mused. "She must have shifted for the first time at fourteen. They shunned her because she's a runt. That's insane. Then that fucker Arik got his hands on her, what, a year or two later?"

The idea of that made me sick. Men who preyed on helpless *children* deserved to die a slow death. Given her age now, he must have had her for nearly a decade.

"Kevin? Boss?" Blake dragged me out of my murderous thoughts.

"Yes. I think you could be right," I said.

Nathaniel's jaw worked so hard that I could hear his teeth grinding together.

Blake stared at the fire. "Once we're done with this wolf pack, I say we hunt down Arik. He deserves it."

I couldn't agree more.

13
GEM

I bolted upright, and immediately regretted the movement when a dull ache overtook my entire body. I felt like I'd been torn apart by wolves. As flashes of memories surfaced of yesterday's events, I realized that I had, in fact, been torn apart by wolves. Yet somehow I survived.

The memories, and my current thudding pain, were overshadowed by my surprise when I looked down at the bed. Kevin slept softly at my side, and on my other side was... Blake.

His blue eyes fluttered open. "How are you feeling, princess?" His voice was thick with sleep. What was he doing here?

I groaned. "I've been better." And worse. Much, much worse.

He rolled over and picked something up from the nightstand. "This is probably kind of cold by now but drink it anyway." He held up a cut of tea and I took it.

A bitter, earthy taste coated my tongue, and I cringed. I took another sip. I'd had this bark tea before and knew it would help with the pain. "Thank you."

He waited for me to finish, then took the empty cup away. By the time he turned back, I lay back down and my eyelids had started to droop, my muscles relaxed. When he looped an arm around me, I snuggled into his warmth.

How did it feel so right to be this close to him?

"Sleep, princess. You'll feel better when you wake up."

The second time I woke, I was alone. I stretched, tentatively checking my wounds and bruised muscles. Stitches pulled at my side so I stopped before they popped open. Easing out of bed, I made my way downstairs to face the bears, my rescuers.

Once again, I replayed what had happened yesterday in my head, imagining what must have happened after I lost consciousness.

My cheeks flamed. They'd finally seen my wolf, the weak and pathetic runt. I was an anomaly among my kind. No one knew what to do with a small she-wolf who never had a chance of standing up for herself. My pack had shunned her, other wolves ridiculed her, even I had abandoned that part of myself and insisted on living as a human. The full moon had held no sway over my instincts for a very long time.

Yesterday had been the first time I'd released my wolf form in forever.

I entered the main floor, expecting to find disgust on Kevin and Blake's faces. Luckily, Nathaniel wasn't there, as his expression would have been the worst of them all. Suddenly, I felt guilty for binding Kevin to me without having told him the full truth about myself. Would he still want me as his mate? A runt wolf was truly worthless.

A quiet, wolfish whine vibrated in my throat. The only kindness fate had ever shown me was with Kevin. I wanted to keep him, though now, I doubted that was possible.

"Good morning, sweetheart." Kevin lifted his head to look at me and his brows crashed down. "What's wrong?"

Blake leaned against the counter with a concerned expression.

I opened my mouth to respond, then snapped it shut. This was not the greeting I'd expected. Where was their disgust? Or their cold shoulder that told me I wasn't worthy of their attention?

My voice came out so low that only a shifter's ears could hear my words. "You saw what I am. You know the truth about my wolf." Unshed tears burned behind my eyes. "Don't you hate me now?"

For such large men, they moved quickly, closing the physical distance between us until I was enveloped in their warmth. Kevin took my face in his hands, while Blake rubbed circles on my back. They wore matching expressions of confusion and concern.

"You've been shunned your whole life for being such a small creature?" Kevin asked.

My cheeks burned with humiliation. I nodded. "I-I'm a wolf who doesn't belong among wolves. I'm pathetic."

Kevin shook his head.

"Don't you ever say that again." Blake's palm slid up my back until his fingers wrapped around the nape of my neck. "And you're right, you don't belong among wolves. You belong with us." His thumb rested against my thundering pulse. "Your wolf is the cutest, most adorable creature I've ever seen."

I blinked up at him, taken aback. "Did you just call me adorable?"

He nodded.

My face fell into a scowl. "Don't mock me." I stepped away from him and Kevin.

"I'm not. You are adorable." One side of Blake's mouth lifted in a smile. "Your tiny wolf makes me want to scoop you up and cuddle you forever. Big bear, little wolf... I can see it. I like it."

I scoffed. "That's not funny—"

Kevin captured my gaze with his warm hazel one. "We're not mocking you. Promise. You have no idea how much your small stature, as both a woman and a wolf, brings out the protective need in us bears. We don't see you as weak. We see you as *ours*."

Years' worth of conditioning and abuse couldn't be wiped away by his words, but they sure helped. My inner wolf, who I, myself, had shunned because of all the grief she'd brought me, perked up. She looked through my eyes at these two giants and liked what she saw.

Mates? The question tumbled around in my head. Kevin kept saying how I belonged to *them,* that I was *theirs*—not just his. He didn't seem to mind Blake's hands on me either.

I craved their attention and their touches... from both of them. But I didn't want to get ahead of myself. A weak, runty wolf such as myself shouldn't even have one fated mate, much less two. *Or three?* a soft voice whispered in my mind. Nathaniel. I inwardly shuddered. Unlike Blake and Kevin, he despised me, and he wasn't afraid to show it.

"Talk to us, sweetheart?" Kevin moved toward me.

I leaned forward, seeking comfort in Kevin's embrace. "You're the first people to see me as something other than a freak, so I'm just trying to process all of this. I've shoved my wolf away for so long that I barely know my own instincts, my own nature. I'm just... lost."

Blake stepped behind me, his heat blanketing my back. "Denying your inner animal never leads to anything good. Just ask Nathaniel."

"What do you mean?" My curiosity was piqued by that vague statement.

"Never mind. But you need to reconnect with your wolf, for both your sakes."

I twisted my head to look at Blake. "How?"

Most of the time, the place she occupied in my chest was hollow, like she'd truly vanished. Today was the first time in years that she was more of a presence. But I doubted she would stay for long.

Because you don't want her, so why would she stay?

If two strong bears could see all of me, and see me as worthy, then maybe I could too. Maybe it was time to give myself, and my wolf, a second chance.

"I have an idea," Kevin said. "But first, you need to eat."

They spent the rest of the day putting me through a series of situations that were supposed to call upon my wolfish instincts. As I summoned my wolf to heighten my senses, she came easier each time. It broke my heart to realize that she sought acceptance from me as much as I did from others.

Once I had that realization, I opened my arms and wholly embraced her. Fate had made me a runt. It wasn't my, or my wolf's, fault. All these years I thought she was what made me weak, but I'd been wrong. She was my only source of true strength.

It was *her* heightened senses, quicker reflexes, and instincts that would have made surviving in this world easier. She took one whiff of these two bears and immediately liked them. She approved of Kevin, especially liking his soft, soothing voice and his intelligent eyes. The gaping age difference between us didn't bother her at all.

She took to Blake quickly as well. She enjoyed his easy smiles and rumbly chuckles. I saw him in a new light through her eyes. He was kind and caring. Asshole Blake was a distant memory at this point.

In all fairness, he was the one in charge of my daily punishment. He couldn't have been all sweet about it or that wouldn't have made any sense. Since the moment he'd seen my scars, Blake the Asshole had all but vanished.

The afternoon turned to early evening. Kevin's last idea included playing hide and seek with a blindfold. So, without my use of sight, I navigated through the cabin, relying on my other senses to find him and Blake.

My wolf's sense of smell was powerful enough to sniff out Blake's citrusy scent. I opened the pantry, amused by the thought of him trying to wedge his large body into such a tight space.

"Got you!" I reached out to tag him, but his fingers gripped my wrist and he pulled me into the pantry with him. I yelped in surprise as the door clicked shut.

"Are you sure you've got me, or have I got you?" His sweet breath washed across my face.

"Well, you're the one hiding and I'm the one seeking. So..." I attempted to remove the blindfold but Blake stayed my hand.

"So? What do your wolf senses tell you right now?" He was so close that our bodies melded together. I felt each rise and fall of his chest against mine.

Leaving the blindfold in place, I let my other senses reach out and explore. My skin prickled from being this close to him. His full, masculine scent floated up my nose and through my head. I swore I could hear the slow thud of his beating heart. He filled my entire sphere, my entire universe, in that moment. I felt a deep desire to take more of him, so I did.

Reaching up, I looped my arms around his neck and wove my fingers through his long, thick hair. With one hand, he cupped my ass and lifted. My legs straddled his waist.

My lips found his, tentatively at first. He tasted of lemon and heat. A low rumble sounded in my throat and I deepened our kiss, my tongue exploring his mouth. He pressed my back against the wall of shelves, neither one of us caring about the rattling cans of food as we ravaged each other.

His cock grew hot and heavy between us, pressing against my damp jean-clad pussy. I wanted him with a need that threatened to swallow me whole.

He broke away. "The mating fever is demanding I take you now."

"Yes. Please," I spoke against his lips.

He let out a soft curse. "You'd let me take you here? Fuck you and claim you while you're blindfolded in a cabinet?"

I swallowed hard. Right now, I'd let him do anything.

He chuckled at my telling silence. "Such a naughty girl."

Was I?

Blake ground his erection against my sensitive clit, and I moaned. I felt like I was going to explode at any moment even though we were both still fully clothed. None of my sexual experiences before coming here had been anything like this. It blew my mind. I wanted all the orgasms, all the time.

He stopped, gripped my hips, and put the tiniest bit of space between us. "You should go find Kevin before his patience wears thin. He's not usually one for games."

His words hit me like a frigid splash of water. Was that a rejection?

Sensing my change in mood, he said, "Don't get me wrong, princess, I want you so badly, I'm seconds away from tearing your clothes off and fucking you until you can't walk." He planted a soft kiss on my lips. "But if this is forever, I want us to both be clearheaded before we take the plunge. You barely know me. You might not like the real *me*."

My brain cleared a little.

"Which version is the real you?" I asked. "Asshole Blake, Caring Blake, or Possessive Blake?"

"All of them."

I thought for a moment. "Did you like punishing me?"

He hummed. "Honestly, part of me took immense pleasure in bossing you around. But now that I think about it, the pleasure came more from being around you all day than making you hurt. Don't get me wrong. I'm no Prince Charming. I think about spanking your gorgeous ass every single day."

"You do?" I wasn't sure how I felt about that idea. Would it feel good, or would it hurt?

"Oh, darling, that's just the beginning of the dirty thoughts I have about you on a daily basis. When you're mine, I'll show you." He nipped my bottom lip. "Can you deal with that?"

"I think so." I loved hearing his filthy promises. "You're wrong about me barely knowing you. I think I have a pretty good idea of who you are. You're passionate, and you wear your emotions on your sleeve."

"Hm. True." He untwined my legs and let me slide down his front until my feet touched the floor. "Now before I'm tempted any further, go find Kevin and give him that soaking wet pussy that smells like heaven."

A sensual tremor racked my body at his command. Why was it so sexy to be told by the man who'd made me all hot and bothered to give myself to his friend? As soon as I found Kevin, he'd know exactly what happened between me and Blake.

The door clicked open.

On wobbly knees, I followed Kevin's spicy, earthy smell upstairs to his room. As soon as I stepped inside, I sensed his presence.

His deep voice came from where he lay on the bed. "You look like a stiff breeze could make you come. Come here, sweetheart, let me give you what you want."

14

GEM

"Where is Nathaniel?" I asked over dinner. Even if one of them was patrolling, they were always back in time for the evening meal. I'd assumed he'd been fulfilling that duty today, but I was beginning to think I was wrong.

"He's tracking the wolves who attacked you," Kevin said.

My lips formed an *O*. "Are they the same ones who've been in your territory before?"

"They are, yes."

"Why... why do you think they attacked me?"

"I don't know exactly," Kevin admitted.

Blake said, "We think they're a pack of outlaws. One of Kevin's old bosses runs a pack for outcasts in the Rocky Mountains. They'll take in any stray. But if these wolves are running wild, my guess is that they are running from something. Probably the law."

"Okay, but why attack me? I don't know any of

them." At least none of the wolves had looked familiar. Would I have picked up on any hint of familiarity through my intense fear? Either way, Arik was the one who pissed people off and owed debts to the worst types, not me.

"They may have realized that you're with us," Kevin spoke softly. "They've been very aggressive about trying to stake their claim on our land. They may have attacked you out of spite. Or to wound us."

That brought a fresh roll of fear over me. "Do you think Nathaniel is okay out there on his own? What if they discover him following them?"

Blake leaned back in his chair, his fingers laced behind his head. "If you knew Nathaniel, you wouldn't worry about him. He's one hard son of a bitch to kill. And if they piss him off enough to flip his switch..." He shrugged. "Then we really won't have to worry about them ever again."

"If he could take out that entire pack, then why hasn't he done it already?" I asked, unsettled by these revelations about Nathaniel.

"Because in order to destroy them all, he'd have to lose control." He leaned forward. "And he hates losing control. So it's not an option."

I shivered from a chill only I could feel. "And you trust him enough to live under the same roof as him?"

Kevin answered me this time. "We trust him with our lives."

Good to know. But did that mean that I should as well?

The full moon crested the treetops, illuminating the forest in a silvery light through the cabin's windows. For the first time in years, I felt the urge to shift. My wolf wanted to howl at the moon. She clawed against my chest, asking to be freed tonight.

"What is it, princess?" Blake asked, noticing my restlessness.

"The moon is full and my wolf wants out."

"Then let her out for a run." He glanced at Kevin. "A run would do us some good too. We'll come with you."

A rush of pleasure went through me. "You will?"

Kevin stood. "Of course we will. Let's let our beasts out for a while."

I followed them outside to the porch, where we quickly stripped down as our breaths fogged in the air. Closing my eyes, I let my wolf take over. She knew what she was doing. Worrying about the agony, holding back the shift, would only make the transformation more painful. Instead, I let go.

My bones and flesh morphed in a matter of seconds. I only had time for a sharp inhale at the start of it before I was standing on all fours. That had been the smoothest shift I'd ever experienced. Maybe I really could do this whole wolf thing.

Two bears stood in place of the men. I bounded around them, feeling even tinier in their mighty presence. With a playful yip, I raced off through the trees.

Beneath my feet, the earth trembled, and I knew my bears were close behind.

I let loose. The wind swept back my fur, my paws indented the soft ground, and my senses came alive to the scents and sounds of nighttime creatures. I ignored their scurrying. I wasn't here to hunt tonight, just to run, to feel freedom in its purest form.

I crossed small meadows, flowing streams, and worked my way up to a ridge that overlooked the valley below. Panting, tongue lulling, I waited for Kevin and Blake to catch up. The view from up here was glorious—nothing but forest and mountains and sky for as far as the eye could see.

Tranquility pumped through my veins. I'd never felt more alive than I did in that moment. This place was beautiful and wild.

Kevin appeared at the tree line first. My chest blossomed with warmth as I recognized my mate, my love. The large brown bear made me feel cherished in a way I hadn't realized was possible before.

When Blake stepped forward, my gaze latched onto him. *Mate?* I cocked my head to one side, evaluating the black bear. He smelled like a mate. Possessiveness filled me, but my logical side couldn't fathom having more than one. My wolf, however, was drawn to him like a moth to a flame.

Kevin had told me I belonged to not only him, but to *them*, yet I found that difficult to believe.

The two bears lumbered toward me. I'd caught my breath and I zoomed around them, playfully snapping and snarling. I was quick compared to their more languid movements. Of course, they weren't actually trying all that hard to catch me.

In an attempt to up the game, I sank my teeth into Blake's furry butt cheek, then darted off through the trees. He released a terrifying roar that promised retribution and came after me. This was it. The chase was on.

I led him in circles and figure eights all over the woods. At one point, he entered a clearing to drink from a narrow stream while I hid behind a fallen tree. His back was to me, so I slowly crept up behind him, noting that the soft breeze carried my scent in the opposite direction and away from him.

When I was close enough, I launched myself into the air and landed on his broad back. My victory was short lived. Blake jerked his shoulders, and I went flying off. I tumbled across the damp grass.

He stalked toward me and I shifted, lying on my back and gazing up at the full moon. By the time Blake got to me, he'd taken on his human form too.

"You bit me on the ass. What kind of wolf are you?" He rubbed his butt, the small wound already healing.

I giggled.

"You think that's funny?" His eyes narrowed. "How would you like it if I bit your ass?"

I lifted onto my elbows to get a better view of him—tanned skin, long black hair draped over his shoulders, and blazing blue eyes that held amusement at my assessing gaze. My eyes dropped lower, taking in powerful muscles and a generously proportional cock.

My throat grew tight, making it difficult to draw in a

full breath. He was absolutely gorgeous awash in the full moon's light.

"Like what you see, princess?" His voice had dropped half an octave. My nipples pebbled, and not from the cool air.

Blake dropped to his knees at my side. "That was a question. Do you like it?" He fisted his now rigid cock, his gaze boring into mine.

I licked my lips and let my eyes drop to his dick. My breath hitched. He seemed to grow larger as he stroked himself. *Fates, it's huge.*

I gaped up at him, and he smirked. Cocky. But I guess he had every right to be, packing that between his legs.

"Speechless, huh?" His grin widened. "I'm sure I can get a noise out of you. How about a little tit for tat?"

He reached for me just as I realized his intention. I squealed and tried to roll away, but his arms were so long, he easily snatched me by the hips. Turning me over, he pinned my body to the ground with one splayed palm, then sunk his teeth into my butt cheek. The bite didn't break skin, but I shrieked anyway.

When he rubbed away the pinching pain, I closed my eyes and moaned. That got me a solid smack on the ass. My skin flushed as the sensation brought more pleasure than pain.

"How do you like that, princess?" he asked, and I answered him with another soft moan. "Is that right? Are you a naughty girl?" He slapped my ass again, then kneaded my flesh. His huge, rough hands, and the way he held me down, made me instantly wet.

I jolted with surprise. Normally being at a male's mercy like this would riddle me with fear, but everything was different with my mates.

Mates, plural.

I tried to turn over onto my back, but Blake kept his hold on me. "Not yet. I'm not done with this sweet ass of yours. You have no idea how long I've wanted to do this to you." He grazed his teeth across my flesh and I shivered. Adjusting his position, he wedged his knee between my legs, spreading my thighs. Then he dipped his fingers into my soaked pussy. A low hum vibrated in his chest.

I whimpered as his fingers filled and stretched me. Only with Kevin had I experienced so much pleasure at a man's hands.

Turning my head, I briefly searched the forest for any sign of my first mate. There, movement caught my eye. Kevin stood in his bear form and watched us. The knowledge that he was there sent a rush of exhilaration through my chest. He stood there silently watching and waiting for me to claim my other mate.

Blake removed his fingers and flipped me over. Capturing my gaze, he brought his digits to his mouth and sucked on his fingers. His eyes rolled back in his head. A low humming sound vibrated in his chest.

"You taste like honey." He lifted my legs over his shoulders. "I want more."

I stared at him in shock when he dipped his head between my legs and kissed my cunt. Adjusting his hold on my hips, he speared me with his tongue. I'd certainly never been tongue-fucked before, but damn did it feel good. I reached up and twisted my fingers in his hair.

Blake used his teeth, tongue, and fingers to make me come on his face. As my orgasm pulsed through me, he bit down, leaving his mark on my inner thigh. This bite did break the skin, and I knew I'd find the outline of his teeth imprinted on my thigh forever.

Even with that, he wasn't done yet. My screams echoed into the night as he made me come twice more. My clit was so sensitive that I begged him to stop.

Eyeing me, he rose onto his knees. "You think you're ready for this?" he asked, palming his heavy length.

The thing looked like it would split me in two, but I nodded. I needed to feel him inside me.

Blake was gentle and cautions as he took his time inching into my pussy. He stretched me in the most unbelievable ways. Rocking his hips, he was eventually seated all the way inside. I was panting from the intensity and trying to keep my muscles relaxed around his girth.

"Are you okay?" he asked, concern etched on his brow.

"Yes. Move. Please." I dug my heels into his ass.

He took the cue and slowly withdrew to the tip before pushing back in. "You're so tight and small. I don't want to break you."

"You won't," I swore, even though I wasn't entirely certain of my own words. At this point, the sensation of him filling me up was somewhere between pleasure and pain. "Give me more."

He curled his fingers around the back of my neck

and kissed me deeply. Pleasure grew out of the burning discomfort. Soon, he was rocking into me as I hung on for dear life. He worked my clit, sending shots of ecstasy straight to my brain. Eventually, I was meeting him thrust for thrust.

Seemingly out of nowhere, another orgasm ripped through me. I was clenching him so hard, he stilled. My inner wolf bared her fangs and marked Blake as our mate on his collarbone.

"I can't hold back," he ground out. Then, he was pounding into me with wild abandon. I gasped, trying to catch my breath. A couple more sporadic thrusts and he found his release. "Fuck!"

Immediately, he froze.

"Did I hurt you?" His gaze searched my eyes.

I smoothed his long black hair away from his face and kissed the tip of his nose. "I'm fine. Stop worrying about me, okay?"

He scrutinized me for half a minute longer. "Are you absolutely sure I didn't hurt you? Because that's the last thing I'd ever want to do."

"I'm sure." I was also sure I would be sore as fuck all day tomorrow, but it was totally worth it. He was *mine*.

BLAKE

Kevin tapped my shoulder, waking me from where I slept with Gem in my bed. We'd been taking turns with her the past few days and last night had been my time alone with our little mate.

Not wanting to wake her, I slipped out of bed as quietly as I could and followed Kevin to his office at the end of the hall.

This space was the opposite of quaint and rustic. High-powered computers hummed, their screens casting an eerie, unnatural glow across his desk. From here, he was in contact with the outside world. And after Gem so easily found her way inside our haven, he'd installed a hefty security system around the cabin.

Massive, nearly silent generators powered this operation. I had no idea where he got all this shit. Whenever I asked him about it, he simply said it was some such contact, or old friend, or a favor from so-and-so. I figured it all came from the syndicate he used to work for.

He poured us each a cup of black coffee from the buffet before launching into why he'd awoken me this early.

"I heard back from Lucas. He told me a pack resembling the one who's been harassing us had been to his outcast haven lands a few months back. They'd wanted a piece of property to call their own. At first, he agreed and set them up in a section of the mountainside, but they soon wore out their welcome." His frown deepened. "That light brown colored Alpha of theirs is called Sven. He's wanted by both the supernatural and human authorities for murder, robbery, and rape. Lucas said there were several unsavory episodes with Sven before he decided to oust them all."

I let out a low whistle. "Shit, boss. This is more serious than we thought."

From what I knew of Lucas, one of Kevin's old bosses, the guy had a soft spot for shunned wolves. He'd basically set up a rescue for lone wolves and those who didn't fit in anywhere else. If he gave them the boot, then they really were bad news.

My gut tightened further. "Gem. Do you realize how much worse their attack on her could have turned out if we hadn't gotten to her when we did?"

He gave a curt nod. "That has crossed my mind too. It's imperative that we keep her safe and out of Sven's hands."

"We need to deal with them. Sooner rather than

later." I set my coffee cup down on the desk. "Where the fuck is Nathaniel?"

"I don't know. He'll return when he has information for us."

I grunted. I was growing impatient with each day that he was gone. We were at a standstill until we knew where to find Sven and his pack—not only where they settled for the night, but their usual hangouts, known associates, everything.

One thing Kevin never did was go into a situation without knowing all the information and thoroughly viewing it from every angle. While that was smart and all, the waiting drove me crazy. Couldn't we just surprise them and take them all out? Why did everything always need a fucking plan?

I supposed my lack of planning was why I'd never been able to settle down until now. And now that I had my mate, I wasn't going anywhere unless it was with her.

"We'll neutralize their threat, Blake. I promise."

Since Kevin always made good on his promises, I heaved a sigh and relaxed a bit. We'd get rid of those fuckers. All in good time—or some shit.

A clanking sound from the kitchen caught my attention. "Sounds like our mate is up and about."

"I need to finish up here. I'll see you downstairs." Kevin focused on one of his computer screens.

I took my coffee cup and strode down to the kitchen, where I was met with the most adorable sight of my life —Gem making breakfast, flour in her hair and smeared across one cheek. She wore one of my T-shirts, and the sight of her sent a possessive thrill straight to my cock.

"What are you up to?" I asked, prowling toward her.

She glanced up with a smile. "Making pancakes."

"Oh yeah?" I stood behind her and buried my nose in her neck. She smelled like dough, strawberries, and sex. I snaked my hand down and cupped her delicious cunt.

Mine.

Okay, yeah I had to share her with Kevin, but that was manageable. In some ways, it was good to know that she had him as well as me to take care of her every want and need.

She squirmed against me, grinding that sweet ass against my throbbing cock. She knew exactly what she was doing—driving me wild. I was so glad she could handle all of me. It took a special kind of woman to do that, and I'd finally found her.

Slipping my fingers under the hem of her shirt, I trailed them up her thigh, and was rewarded with a shiver.

"How about we put breakfast on hold? I want a different kind of meal first." Spinning her in my arms, I lifted her onto the kitchen counter and sank to my knees. I spread her thighs and dove in like a man starved. She gasped at the sudden intrusion.

Fuck, she tasted good. I could eat her out all day long.

It wasn't long before she was moaning, her thighs quivering. Suddenly, her body tensed and she screamed my name.

I grinned. Now that was the sweetest sound in the world.

Footsteps pounded down the stairs and Kevin appeared. "What—" he cut himself off, taking in our positions, and Gem's flushed face. "I see."

He stood at the base of the stairs, studying us with a thoughtful expression. He looked torn between stepping closer and retreating up to the second floor.

"Join us," Gem blurted. More color rose in her cheeks. "Is that... okay?" she asked me.

I stood, struck by a sudden idea, and whispered in her ear. "Do you want some cock in your mouth, princess? Want to suck on him while I fuck you from behind?"

"Y-yes," she said breathily.

I turned to Kevin. "Sit down."

His brow pinched. He wasn't used to taking orders from me. His gaze fell on Gem, who nodded, so he settled in one of the dining table chairs.

Gem lifted the T-shirt over her head and tossed it aside as she walked up to him. She fell to her knees in front of Kevin, and I had to admit, the sight was hot as fuck. Undoing his fly, she took him into her mouth.

Kevin fisted her hair and groaned. "That's a good girl, swallow me whole. Just like that."

Fucking hell.

I dropped my jeans and kneeled behind Gem. Taking her hips, I angled her ass upward so I could bury my cock in her tight pussy. Each thrust into her made her gag on Kevin's dick. We worked in tandem, fucking her mouth and her pussy.

She felt so good that it was challenging for me to keep a level head. I wanted to fuck her into oblivion, but I held back.

When I couldn't take any more, I pinched her clit. She came so hard on my cock, I let out a string of curses. Kevin laughed until she screamed and he lost control with a curse of his own. The sight of him fucking her face and coming down her throat was enough to shatter my control.

I slammed into her over and over. "You take my cock so well, like your pussy was fucking made for it." A few more wild strokes and I came undone. I pumped so much cum into her that it leaked down her thighs. Satisfied, I rested my head against her back.

It took a minute for the three of us to catch our breaths. I pulled out and zipped up my jeans. Kevin cradled Gem's head in his lap and tucked her hair behind her ear. She was a vision, sated, naked, and ours.

I smacked her ass. "I'll make the pancakes, but you're eating them at the table naked."

Kevin's eyes shone with amusement. "I second that motion."

It was settled. I did make pancakes, and we ate our fill, which led to a round of sex on the dining table, a couple of broken dishes, and syrup in some unusual places. Needless to say, it was a well spent morning, that turned into an equally productive afternoon.

16

GEM

"**C**ome out, come out, wherever you are, little wolf," Blake taunted me. I was pretty sure he knew exactly where I was hiding and just pretending he couldn't find me. Although, I could fit into much smaller spaces than he could, so maybe it wasn't obvious.

I held back a giggle as he made another pass through the kitchen area. When he was right below my hiding spot on top of the upper cabinets, I launched myself at him, free falling onto his broad shoulders.

He whirled around in time to catch me, but my momentum had him staggering backward. He crashed into the wooden table with a curse. I took advantage of his distraction by climbing further up his chest and wrapping my legs around his neck. On his momentarily unsteady feet, it was all I needed to fell this giant.

His back hit the floor. "*Oof.*"

I snapped and snarled at him when he tried to toss

me off. My thighs were like a vice around his neck and I wasn't letting go until he surrendered. A wide grin split his face, and I knew I was in trouble. With a squeal, I leaped off him, preparing to run while he gave chase.

The front door burst open. "What the fuck is going on in here?" Nathaniel snarled.

I growled at him, shocking everyone in the room, including myself.

The big blond bear glared at me. I glowered back, unfazed.

Blake got up and came to my side. "We're just playing around."

That explanation brought a deeper scowl to Nathaniel's face.

"You're back. You must have news. One sec." Blake called up the stairs for Kevin. "Nathaniel's back!"

We all moved toward the dining table and, a moment later, Kevin joined us.

Nathaniel dragged a hand through his dirty hair. "I followed them around in circles for a few days. I think they were trying to be careful and make sure no one was tailing them, but they never lost me.

"They finally settled down in an encampment a couple of valleys over from here, further to the east. It's forest service property so they mostly go unnoticed, but they don't own that land. It seems they like this area, and three bears may seem easier to run off than another entire wolf pack. I think that's why they're after our land specifically."

Blake chuckled. "The last thing we are is easy to bully off our own land. Stupid fuckers."

That was true. From what I'd learned of my bears, they were stubborn and dangerous enough that no one who had any sense would mess with them.

Kevin took a moment to mull over everything Nathaniel had said. "Did you see the pale brown Alpha?"

Nathaniel nodded. He carefully avoided my gaze. It was like old times; him pretending I didn't exist.

"We have confirmation that his name is Sven. Lucas had issues with him a few months ago…"

I didn't catch the rest of what Kevin said because my mind latched on to that name—*Sven*. Why did it sound so familiar? Since I'd spent almost the past decade of my life with Arik, he was the most likely connection. But was Sven a business associate or a rival? They were both Alpha wolves, so it could go either way. The mention of Sven's name did bring up my wolf's hackles. What did she know about him?

I voiced my concerns. "I think Sven knows Arik. What if Sven saw and attacked me not because of you guys but because he's one of Arik's rivals and he recognized me as Arik's old girlfriend?"

Nathaniel eyed me like I was intruding on their private conversation. *Suck it, Mr. Sour-face.* I'd spent the past two weeks here with my mates, reconnecting with my wolf, and I felt a million times changed from the last time Nathaniel had been home.

"I suppose that's possible," Kevin admitted. "Whatever Sven's motivations, you don't have to worry about it. We'll protect you from him and his pack."

I smiled at him and Blake. "I know. But wouldn't it

be good to know what his motivations are, besides the obvious?"

Kevin bobbed his head. "I have my contacts digging a bit deeper into Sven and his pack. I'll look into his connection with Arik."

I sighed in relief. The last thing we needed was for this battle over my bears' land to go from a property challenge to a personal vendetta. Arik was terrible, but the people he made his enemies were far, far worse. Though I could say the same about his friends.

"What's the plan, boss?" Nathaniel asked. He looked tired with circles under his icy-green eyes and smudges of dirt on his skin.

"We know where their main camp is now. I need some more information, and I'm going to call in a couple of favors. Until then, we wait."

Blake groaned. Kevin shot him a look that shut him up.

Nathaniel's green gaze flicked briefly to me before settling on Kevin. "So, what's been going on around here? You know what, hold that thought. I need a fucking shower." He stood and strode to the main floor bathroom. We watched until he closed the door behind him, then I glanced at my two mates.

"How are we going to tell him that we've all, um, you know?" I waved my hand between the three of us.

Blake laughed. "Trust me, he already knows."

Kevin's nod confirmed Blake's statement.

Huh. Well, Nathaniel's addition to our little love nest was sure to mix things up. He obviously hated my guts, so how long was he going to be okay sticking around while the three of us continued our relationship?

Did this mean no more kitchen sex? Hell, he'd probably wash the table with bleach if he knew what we'd done all over it a couple of days ago. I chewed on my thumbnail, uncertainty of the future settling in my stomach.

17

GEM

During the next few days, we fell into a rhythm of household chores, eating our meals together, and Nathaniel and I doing our best to ignore each other. My nights were spent with one or both of my mates.

My wolf kept her eye on Nathaniel as if he were a particularly interesting specimen. I urged her to ignore him like I did, but she wouldn't listen. She was intrigued by him, but I didn't know why. Lurking beneath that tousled-blond hair and gorgeous, scowling face was a dangerous beast.

I mentally went over the snippets of insight I'd gotten from Blake. Nathaniel kept a tight rein on his darker side and was dangerous when he lost control. Instinctively, I knew he was lethal. His edginess told me he was more dangerous than Blake and Kevin combined, and that was almost... impressive.

So, I tried to avoid him.

Which I succeeded in doing until one afternoon when I rounded the cabin and spotted a shirtless Nathaniel chopping wood. His body glistened with sweat. My gaze trailed over his broad, muscular back, and down his tattooed arms.

Mate? my inner wolf asked.

Absolutely not.

She sulked.

What a horny bitch. *Not every attractive bear shifter on the planet is our mate.*

Besides, I already had two. *Two.* Double that of most shifters, and I certainly did not need Nathaniel. I didn't want him either. Just like he most certainly didn't want me.

Before I had the good sense to tear my eyes away from him, he turned and locked gazes with me. Fury, and something even darker flashed in his cold eyes.

While I didn't want to fuck him, he had lived here before I came along, and he was friends with my mates. The least we could do was be friends, or at least friendly. Obviously he wasn't going to make an effort in that department so it was up to me to try.

Holding his gaze, I walked up to him. "I can help you stack this when you're done, if you'd like."

His eyes narrowed further.

I took an involuntary step back.

He dropped the axe and advanced on me. My heartbeat picked up its pace as I walked backward until he had me pinned against the woodshed. His long fingers wrapped around my neck and my eyes widened when he squeezed.

"You need to understand one thing about me, *honey*." His tone was condescending and edged with danger. "I'm not a nice guy like Blake and Kevin. I *enjoy* inflicting pain." He lowered his head so he could speak into my ear. "I'm getting fucking hard right now just seeing the fear in your big blue doll eyes. So if you know what's good for you, you'll stay the fuck away from me." As if to drive home his point, he flexed his hips so that his erection slid against my stomach.

My heart hammered wildly, but it wasn't fear pulsing through my veins. It was a mixture of arousal and rage.

I lifted my hand and shoved hard at his chest. The impact must have caught him by surprise because his grip loosened around my neck and he took half a step back.

"Don't fucking tell me what to do," I snarled. "I'm not afraid of you." *Though maybe I should be.*

My words hung between us. *Truth or lie?* He was the fucking expert, so he could tell me. He must have decided that I was telling the truth because he said, "You're stupider than I thought."

"And you're a cliché." When all he did was scowl at me, I continued, "Big, tattooed bad boy? Come on." I lowered my voice to mimic his. "*I like pain.*"

"I didn't say that. I said I enjoyed *inflicting* pain."

"Whatever."

Just when I thought his demeanor couldn't get any broodier, his eyes darkened to a deep, intense green. Every muscle in his body went rigid.

Maybe poking the bear hadn't been the best idea.

But I didn't care. I was so tired of being treated like a piece of trash, and being bullied, and seen as *less than*.

"We're all fucked up in some way, Nathaniel. You can't hide from it or, as in your case, use it as a shield forever." That was one lesson I learned so far in my time here.

Nathaniel's hold tightened around my neck, cutting off my air flow. His eyes blazed with fury and for a moment, I thought he was going to snap my neck. He was powerful enough to do it with one quick jerk.

Instead, he abruptly let me go and stalked away into the surrounding trees.

I panted, catching my breath, adrenaline making me jittery. Had I grown too bold? I wasn't sure what had come over me recently, but it was like a floodgate had been opened and I couldn't stop myself from speaking my mind. All the years of suppression, all the pent-up rage, were pouring out of me. If I wasn't careful, my newfound courage was going to get me into trouble.

I completed my original mission, grabbing some dried herbs from the potting shed, and returned to the cabin. Blake greeted me with a smile that faded as he eyed my throat.

Shit. Nathaniel must have left marks on my skin.

"What happened?" he asked.

"Nothing."

"It was Nathaniel, wasn't it?"

I nodded.

"That son of a bitch!" he snarled.

Setting the herbs on the counter, I placed my hands on his chest. "It's fine."

"No. It's not." His jaw tensed. "I'm going to shred him."

Blake made for the door, and I turned to Kevin. "Will you stop him? Please?"

Kevin considered it for a moment, then shook his head. "No. Nathaniel needs to learn that he can't hurt you without repercussions."

I frowned at his back as he continued to chop vegetables. "I don't want anyone to get hurt."

"They'll both be fine." He glanced over his shoulder at me. "Come here. Let me have a look at the damage."

I did as he asked. His shoulders tensed as he brushed my hair aside for a closer look. "If Blake doesn't kill him for this, I just might."

I caught his hand in mine. "It's okay. Really. I think I hurt him more than he hurt me."

Kevin frowned in confusion at my response. I leaned into his chest and wrapped my arms around him.

"It's getting tense around here. I think we all need a break, or a vacation, or something," I said.

He enveloped me in his embrace. "You're right. We'll go to town for the weekend."

The four of us trudged through the forest toward the old logging road. The snow had given way to springtime rain and budding plants. As much as I loved the wilderness, I was looking forward to seeing civilization again.

Near the road stood a well-hidden garage with a single, old pickup truck inside. Blake tossed our bags into a secure container in the truck's bed. We were staying in town for four days and three nights.

Kevin hopped in front of the steering wheel, Blake slid into the middle part of the bench seat then foisted me into his lap, and Nathaniel scooted into the last spot and closed the door.

Immediately, the air thickened with all three men in such a cramped space. I was surprised when Nathaniel said he wanted to come with us. For the past couple of days, following the incident by the woodshed, and his fight with Blake over it, Nathaniel had been quieter than usual.

The truck sputtered to life with a deep rumble, then we were cruising down the mountain toward a resort town that was about two hours away. The ride was bumpy, and every time my arm brushed against Nathaniel's, he'd shoot me a glare. Oof, it was going to be a long trip.

Blake wasn't helping the awkward situation, as all the bouncing of my ass against his crotch was making him hard, which in turn had my thoughts wandering to our sexual encounters. I did my best to ignore the growing heat between my legs by watching the scenery go by the window.

My efforts were dashed when we hit a particularly rough patch of road, and a soft moan escaped my throat. Fucking hell, did this truck have no shock absorbers or whatever those things were called?

Nathaniel's nostrils flared. "For fuck's sake, can't you two keep it in your pants for more than a minute?"

"We're newly mated," Blake drawled, his arms tightening around my waist. "What the fuck do you think?"

Nathaniel grumbled something unintelligible and turned further toward the window.

To say the rest of the ride was excruciating would be an understatement. But we made it to our destination, only to be met with an unfortunate turn of events.

"What do you mean there's been a mix up with our reservation?" Kevin's tone was cool and lethal.

The receptionist cowered. "I'm so sorry. I'm not sure how that happened, but all of our châteaus are occupied, and you're not likely to find anything else in town this weekend because of the holiday celebrations."

Kevin's jaw flexed. "What do you have available that could possibly sleep four?"

The poor guy typed away on his computer, his complexion paling further when he said, "The honeymoon suite is the only room large enough to accommodate you all."

"We'll take it."

With that, we were given keys and made our way to the honeymoon suite. As soon as I stepped inside, my heart sank. The room was huge, decorated in a rustic romantic style. At the far wall stood the centerpiece—the one and only, ridiculously large bed. Sure, we could all fit on that all right, but it was going to be awkward as hell. This room offered absolutely no privacy. Even the huge soaking tub was situated in a corner overlooking the view.

My gaze slid to Nathaniel's, who glared in response. I swore it was his only expression.

I searched for a pullout sofa bed, or anything else, not that it made that much difference, considering we were all going to sleep in one bedroom. In front of the television was a loveseat and a couple of chairs.

Well shit.

18

GEM

After settling into our room as comfortably as we could, we got all dressed up and went out to a swanky dance club where Kevin had reserved us a table in the VIP section. I had to admit, seeing these three bears wearing suits just about undid me. We'd been at the club for a good half hour and my gaze still lingered on them. Well, on Kevin and Blake mostly, Nathaniel managed to still look surly, just better dressed.

I finally had a reason to wear that blue silk dress they bought for me a while ago. With my hair pinned up, the mating mark on my neck was fully visible, two facing crescents.

I sat in the semi-circular booth between Kevin and Blake, each of them resting a possessive hand on my thighs. We drank our first round of drinks and watched people dance on the VIP level dance floor. After a while, I began to sway to the music.

Our server reappeared. She was tall and busty, wearing the plunging top and black short shorts uniform of the waitstaff.

"Would everyone like a second round of drinks?" she asked, hovering close to Blake's side.

Kevin nodded. "We'll take the same as before."

"Sounds great. Can I get you anything else?" She leaned down slightly, just enough to put her tits in Blake's direct line of sight.

"That will be all," Blake said, his eyes never leaving her face.

"Then I'll be right back with your drinks."

I narrowed my gaze at her swaying hips as she walked away. I didn't like the way she was crowding Blake. Though in her defense, I was one woman sitting at a table with three men. Even so, if she kept it up, I'd have to make the situation clearer to her.

She returned a few minutes later and set our cocktails on the table. "Anything else?" Her palm landed on Blake's shoulder.

A low, threatening growl rose from my throat, and her eyes widened.

"Get your hand off my man," I said in a clipped tone.

She snatched her hand back like she'd been burned. "I'm sorry. I thought you were with—"

"They're *all* mine." Another growl rumbled in my chest.

"Oh. *Oh*." She glanced at Blake and Kevin, their expressions amused, then at Nathaniel's deep scowl. "Well, aren't you a lucky girl? Again, I apologize. I didn't realize."

I relaxed a little at her apology. She shot me a wink then moved on to serve another table.

Blake chuckled. "Feeling a bit possessive?"

I rolled my eyes. "Like you wouldn't do the same if some random dude touched me."

"You're right." His thumb stroked the inside of my thigh.

Kevin took my hand in his. "Except we'd do much worse than tell them off."

His dark words sent a shiver down my spine.

I took a sip of my apple martini and smiled at the sweet tanginess. I loved cocktails, and people, and music. My skin tingled with the thrill of being out at a club. I'd been to several before, whenever Arik was trying to impress an associate, but it had never felt like this. Tonight, I felt safe with my two mates and inspired by the unexpected turn of my fate. This was *fun*. There was no ulterior motive to us being here.

"Want to dance?" Blake asked.

I beamed up at him and nodded.

"Come on." He took my hand, and we slid out of the booth and merged with the crowd. Blake towed us to the middle of the dance floor, then spun me around so that my back was to his chest. His arms caged me in as we began to sway to the beat.

Heaven. That's what this felt like.

I rested my head back on his chest and closed my eyes. The floor vibrated under our feet, lights flashing through my eyelids, and all I could feel was his body pressed against mine.

"Happy?" he spoke into my ear.

I looped an arm around the back of his neck. Turning my head, I met his blue gaze. "Ecstatic."

"Good, because this is what our future looks like together." He pressed a soft kiss to my lips. "Fucking in the woods, fucking in a dark corner of this club, and me fucking loving you."

My breath caught in my lungs. My gaze searched his, and I saw the depths of his adoration. "I love you, too." A fluttering sensation erupted in my stomach.

This time, our kiss was more heated yet soft. It promised devotion, happiness, and desire for all eternity. Never in a million years had I thought I'd find love. Yet now, there was no doubt in my mind that I loved both Blake and Kevin. They completed my life in a way that just made sense.

Sure we were fated to each other, but that was only the beginning. What we did, and how we lived our lives as mates, was up to us. And I was lucky enough to find not only my mates, but my soulmates.

We danced for the better part of an hour as one song blended into the next.

"How did you end up sharing a cabin with Kevin and Nathaniel?" I asked.

"Us bachelor bears like to stick together." He turned me to face him and I looped my arms around his neck, as his arms circled my waist. "I've always been a bit of a free spirit, roaming all over, and getting myself into plenty of trouble. Those two helped me out of a tricky situation and... I dunno, I never left. Now they're my family."

"What about your birth family?"

He shook his head. "They're gone. It was just me, and Mom, and Pop growing up. They had gotten together later in life, so they passed when I was in my second year at the academy."

"I'm sorry." Losing family sucked, no matter how it happened. I thought back to my own parents and my little sister. While my parents had shunned me, which left a deep wound in my soul, I would forever miss my sister. "Were you close?"

"We were. Which is partly why I think I didn't settle down or form any other long-term bonds for a while. They were my people, and once they were gone, I just floated for a long time, until I met those two." He glanced over at our booth, where Kevin and Nathaniel were deep in conversation.

"And got into a bunch of trouble along the way?" I asked, amused.

He shrugged. "I've never been accused of being levelheaded, that's for sure."

I huffed a laugh. Blake was passionate about everything he did. I could see that resulting in some interesting situations. I was so glad he had his friends to rely on—and now me as well.

"I'm going to run to the restroom." I spotted the sign over a darkened hallway.

"I'll come with you." He took my hand in his.

I laughed. "That's not necessary. It's right there. I'll be quick."

"I hate letting you out of my sight."

"I'll be fine." I patted his arm. "I'll meet you back at the table. Will you get me some water? I'm parched."

"Fine. Be quick." He moved toward the bar, and I headed in the direction of the bathrooms. The hall was longer, and darker, than it originally appeared. I passed a couple of unmarked doors before arriving at the ladies' restroom near the end. Slipping through the door, I peed, washed my hands, and fixed some stray hairs that had escaped from their pins.

This was my new life. Blake loved me. He'd said those three little words that I'd always longed to hear and never thought I would. My heart grew so light I thought it might float right out of my chest.

Satisfied with my appearance, I exited to the hall-way, and ran into a wall of muscle that suddenly blocked my path. A quick inhale told me everything I needed to know about this person.

I cringed away, but Arik gripped my arms, hard, and shoved me back into the dark corner.

"Gem, I thought that was you."

"What are you doing here?" I asked, frantically trying to determine his mood. The last time I'd seen him, he'd literally dumped me out of his car, thrown away like an empty bag of fast food.

"You know, business as usual. Lots of fine pickings in a rich resort town like this one." He smiled, and I finally registered the dark suit he wore, with his shaggy blond hair slicked back. He was dressed to impress one of his marks, or a client. Either way, it didn't concern me any longer. "The real question is what are *you* doing here?"

I licked my lips. "I'm just here with some friends."

"You don't have any friends." His words bit into me.

"Things change."

He leaned in. "No they don't. I heard you were shacked up with three woodsmen. Do all three of them fuck you? Do they touch what's mine?"

I recoiled. "I'm *not* yours. In fact, I never belonged to you."

"Wrong," he growled. "I'm the only person you'll ever belong to, and if I can't have you, no one will. I realize now that it was a mistake to let you go. You belong with me." He crowded closer, his grip bruising my upper arms. "Don't even think about warning your new masters. You be good and come quietly, or I'll kill everyone close to you. You hear me?"

I glared up at him. "Fuck you."

His eyes widened with shock. "The fuck you say to me?"

"Since you're deaf, I'll repeat myself. I said, go fuck yourself, you useless piece of shit." I spat in his face.

His expression grew stormy. "You're going to regret that."

He lifted his fist, and I instinctively squeezed my eyes closed, bracing for the blow that caught me across my cheekbone. That whole side of my face exploded with agony.

"If you don't want something very bad to happen to your little sister, then you'll keep your mouth shut about me."

I opened my tearing eyes. My sister? What did—?

Arik held up his phone. On the screen was a picture of a pretty blond crossing a street. She was completely oblivious to the person snapping photos of her.

All my bravado crumbled.

Jewels would be seventeen years old now. She looked healthy and happy in that picture. If Arik got his hold on her, he'd ruin her, just like he'd tried to do to me.

Arik shook me. "Am I getting through to you yet?"

I blinked up at him. "How—"

"How, what? How do I have this picture of your sister? I have eyes and ears everywhere, you stupid bitch. Haven't you learned that by now?" He leaned closer. "Now start walking. You're coming with me. Remember, if you make a sound, all I have to do is send one text message and they'll snatch your sister. Now—" A golden, wolfish glow shone in his eyes as he pulled back to sniff the air. "Fuck."

He released me and darted to the emergency exit door. He was gone.

Momentary relief flooded me. I glanced around to figure out what had scared him off when he'd been determined to take me with him. For a moment, the whole situation seemed surreal, and I thought I'd imagined the entire encounter.

Then my gaze landed on a figure at the end of the hallway. Nathaniel's deadly expression told me he'd seen at least part of our exchange. He ambled toward me, freezing me in place with his frosty green eyes.

"I smell an unfamiliar wolf," he said in a flat tone. "Who were you just talking to?"

Arik's threat replayed in my mind. If I wanted to keep my sister safe, I'd say nothing. Arik knew people, bad people, the kind who would do terrible things to my innocent sister.

On the other hand, I knew this wasn't over. Arik had just shown his hand. His plan was to find me and take me back with him. If I knew one thing about him, it was that he never gave up once he set his sights on something he wanted. The bears were my only defense against Arik. Even so, how could I risk Jewels' life for my own? No, I couldn't do that to her.

Even though it had been years since I'd last seen her, that photo brought everything back so vividly, it felt like yesterday. I remembered the sound of her laugh, her easy smiles, and bright, innocent eyes.

We used to pick wildflowers together. I'd taught her how to make daisy chains, and she became a total fiend, weaving and wearing them every day in the spring. She'd made me a dandelion crown once. Jewels was full of life.

I would never take that away from her.

"N-no one," I finally whispered.

Fury flashed in Nathaniel's eyes. "I really hate being lied to. And you, Gem, are a terrible liar. Now you're going to pay the price."

19

NATHANIEL

Her lips parted in response to my threat. Was I really going to punish her for lying to me? Yes. But first I was going to get the truth out of her, one way or another. Taking her arm, I walked her along the hall, opened an unmarked door, and shoved her through. We entered a dimly lit passage with numerous doors along both walls.

I found an unoccupied one, indicated by the steady green light, and swiped my club card that let us into the quiet space. Few people knew about these private rooms available to VIP guests of this club. It wasn't large, but there was space enough for a sofa, low table, and a bar cart. One wall and the ceiling were mirrored, ensuring that the user of this room could fully appreciate their experience here.

"What are you doing?" she demanded, taking in the space with a wary expression. "Blake will be looking for me."

I let out a dark laugh. "No he won't. When you didn't return right away, I volunteered to come find you. They know you're with me."

"And they're not worried about that?" She frowned.

"They don't have a choice." I was annoyed at her for hiding behind them. She was mine just as much as she was theirs. It was time I made her realize that truth.

The line between her brows deepened in confusion. "What do you mean—"

I pounced on her, gripping both of her wrists in one hand, and pinning her against the door. She yelped in surprise, then leveled me with a glare. I liked it when she was feisty.

"You're not getting out of here until you tell me the truth. So you better start talking."

I could see her mind working. She was debating, torn. But why?

"If you don't start talking, I'm going to bend you over my knee and spank your ass raw." I tugged up on her wrists, stretching her body taut against the door. I noticed the marks on her arms, and the faint bruising on her cheekbone.

Fury crawled through my gut. "Who did this to you?" I trailed my fingers over the bruises.

Panic blotted out the fire in her eyes. "No one."

"Stop. Lying." The thought of someone hurting her like this made my control slip. "Who the fuck did this to you?"

She flinched, but said, "I'm not afraid of you."

"I know you think that. If you keep avoiding my

question, I'm going to change your mind. And I'll enjoy doing it," I growled.

She arched her back just enough to press her breasts flush against my chest. "I think you're all talk and no bite."

"Oh honey, you have no idea." I stepped in until every inch of her body was molded to mine. Fuck, she felt good. "Who. Was. It?"

Her frown returned full force. "He threatened to kidnap and hurt my sister if I said anything to anyone. He came for me and wanted me to go quietly with him."

My inner beast snarled. No one was taking her from me—from us.

Her words rang true. I could easily guess who this mystery man was, but just to be sure...

"Arik?" I asked.

"Yes." Her expression tightened with worry. "He's going to hurt my sister. Jewels is only seventeen."

I inwardly cursed. Releasing her, I fished my phone from my pocket and sent a text to Kevin.

Gem hugged herself as she watched me. "What are you doing?"

"Letting the guys know what's going on. They'll find Arik and deal with him."

"I don't want to get Kevin and Blake hurt." She chewed on her thumbnail.

I snorted, then studied her for a long moment. "You're serious. You actually think Arik is a threat to them?"

"What? Of course I do. Arik knows people. Killers and worse. If he wants you dead, then he'll make it happen. I just never thought he'd try to get me back. Now we're all in trouble. I need to get out of here."

I blocked her escape, caging her body against the wall with mine.

"Your concern is so *touching*," I sneered. "But you're staying right here while they deal with this. Believe me, we are the last people you have to worry about. You know those *killers*, and the other people that you're so afraid of? We're worse than them. I guarantee it." My hand swept into her hair and fisted it. She gasped. Her pulse quickened, and I resisted the urge to lick the throbbing vein in her neck. "If you only knew how much blood was on my hands alone... You wouldn't dare look me in the eye."

"You won't hurt me." She said it like she actually believed those words.

Silly girl.

"I can, and I'll enjoy it. Do you think I'm really so different from the men who gave you those scars?"

Her throat bobbed with a hard swallow. "Yes. You're n-nothing like them," she said, but her eyes held doubt. She was finally starting to understand that she might be wrong about me. "Why did you bring me in here?"

"To punish you for lying to me, remember?" My cock was already growing hard as I imagined all the things I could do with her in this room. We had the time. Kevin and Blake would neutralize the situation. Only then would they come get us from this secure room.

"But I told you what you wanted to know. I told you the truth. Now let me go." Her voice was steady, but some of the spark had left her.

I spoke one simple word into her ear. "No."

A tremor ran through her body. Good.

Pulling away, I gazed into her gorgeous face. "You may have eventually told me the truth, but that doesn't negate the fact that first you lied to me."

Her breath hitched. "What are you going to do to me?"

"Whatever I fucking please." I rocked my dick against her stomach, showing her how hard I was, how serious I was. I'd held back for long enough. Tonight, I would uncage my beast.

Her eyes narrowed, the spark returning. "I'm not going to make it easy for you."

I grinned. "I would hope not. The more difficult you are to break, the more fun it will be for me." I released her hair and instead gripped the front of her dress. One brutal tug was all it took to tear the silky fabric from her delicious curves. Her outraged shriek was music to my ears.

I tore away every shred until she stood before me in a pair of black lace panties and high heels. Much better.

Her breasts rose and fell with breaths of rage, her pink nipples peaked and ready for the taking. "I *liked* that dress, you asshole."

I smirked. Letting her go, I moved to the bar cart to pour myself a bourbon. We were going to be here for a while, why not get comfortable?

I swirled the amber liquid around in my glass before downing it in one go. I reveled in the slow burn all the way down my throat. I turned away from Gem to refill my drink.

Suddenly, searing pain trailed down my back, accompanied by the rip of tearing fabric. I spun, finding Gem holding a strip of my suit coat and shirt in one clawed hand. The skin on my back burned like she'd sliced into me.

She bared her teeth in a feral smile. "Two can play at this game, you scowling jerk."

"You want to play, little wolf-girl?" I surveyed her, amused, and slightly surprised by her metal. We'd see how long she lasted.

"Yeah, I want to play." A golden glow shone in her eyes. Her wolf was out, fangs bared, and ready for a fight. "You're *mine*."

The word *mine* hit me low in the stomach. Somehow, I didn't think she meant it as in *my ass was hers*, but rather as a claiming. Was she fucking claiming me for herself? That was supposed to be my job. I was in charge here. Tonight *I* was claiming *her,* not the other way around.

So, I corrected her. "No, you're mine."

A growl tumbled from her lips. She looked so beautiful nearly naked, clawed fingers smeared with my blood, snarling at me like she hated my guts.

Mate, my inner bear insisted. I rolled my eyes at him. If I let him out, this would be over before it began. Yes, she was our mate, but that didn't mean I had to like it. Nor would it change how I liked to treat and use any woman who was unfortunate enough to stumble into my bed. Gem was no different.

I tore off my shredded suit jacket and the shirt

beneath. Buttons flew across the room and rolled under the sofa, never to be seen again.

I crossed the room, then caught her up in my arms. She wrapped her legs around my waist and ground her hot cunt against my erection. I fisted her hair, tilted her head to the side, and sucked on the side of her neck, right over her thundering pulse, hard enough to leave a mark.

Her teeth sunk into my chest near my collarbone and I jerked back, startled by the pinch of pain. What a devilish little minx. She surprised me further by holding my gaze as her tongue darted out and lapped up the blood from my wound.

Fucking fates, this woman is going to be my undoing.

Holding her still, I devoured her with a scorching kiss. Our tongues dueled, we nipped at each other's lips, and our breaths mingled in a fight for dominance. It didn't seem to matter to her that I was four times her size. She wasn't giving in.

She raked her claws across my back, deep enough to sting. I retaliated by spanking her ass. The result only pushed her pussy further onto my dick that strained against my trousers.

I backed up until my legs hit the sofa, then sat down. Gem immediately popped the button on my slacks, lowered the zipper, and palmed my throbbing cock. I groaned, tilting my head back. I wanted to spill my cum inside her, but I had barely gotten to the punishment I'd promised. So I picked her up and draped her across my lap.

"Remember when I said there would be consequences for lying to me?" I didn't wait for her response. "This is it." My palm cracked across her butt cheeks. She jolted. I did it again, and again until her ass wore my handprints.

She let out a sobbing cry. "*Please.*"

"You had enough?" I rubbed at her burning flesh. "Have you learned your lesson?"

"No," she said in a hushed tone. "Please."

I spanked her again, and she cried out. Moving my fingers lower, I slipped them under her panties to find her sopping wet. *Fuck me.* I pushed a finger into her pussy, stroking her. When she pushed back on my hand, I added another digit. She was so wet and ready to take me.

With my free hand, I smacked her ass again, and felt her cunt flutter as she cried out. Her orgasm shocked the shit out of me. She fucking *liked* this. No, she was reveling in it. She... was fucking unbelievable.

Gem sat up, showing me her flush, tear-stained face. Gorgeous. So fucking pretty.

I slipped my fingers out of her pussy. She straddled my lap, then sunk down on my cock. We both moaned. She started to move first, riding my dick as she chased her next release. She was taking charge—again.

I couldn't have that.

I gripped her waist and plunged up into her tight pussy with enough force to render a gasp. Taking over, I fucked her with brutal force from below, while she clung to my shoulders.

My control snapped. I let go like I'd never dared to before. I'd always fucked hard, brutally. Most of the women I'd been with could handle the pain that was followed with pleasure. Some of them tolerated it enough, but none of them reacted like Gem. None of them tore me apart in return.

Until this moment, I hadn't realized how much I'd kept a tight leash on my restraint. Gem snapped that leash in two and I was free falling. Yet, somehow, I knew she would be there to catch me.

"More," she grunted.

Fucking hell, how could I give her more? As it was, she wouldn't walk right for a week. Blake was going to kill me.

I shoved the thought of him from my mind.

I leaned Gem backward until I could pop one of her nipples into my mouth. I rolled it between my teeth and she shuddered. I slowed my pace, pulling nearly all the way out of her before slamming back into the hilt. She was so tiny, the movement racked her body.

I moved on to her other nipple, giving it the same method of torture, which earned me Gem's claws digging into my forearms. When I bit down on her nipple, she came apart in my arms as her second orgasm seized her body.

Kicking the trousers off the rest of the way, I switched up our positions so that she was beneath me on the sofa. This piece of furniture was built for fucking, wide enough to accommodate two, and sturdy enough for the strength of a shifter.

Her petite form under me would have seemed breakable, except for the way she was shredding my back and matching each of my ruthless thrusts with her own.

My teeth elongated. *Mate, mate, mate.* The chant streamed relentlessly through my mind, but I refused to give in to it. This was borderline hate-fucking, and I wasn't going to claim her as my own like this. She didn't even *like* me. Though I guess, what was there to like?

Sadist.

Torturer.

Killer.

After this night, I was going to have to add *masochist* to my list of identifiers. The pain she caused me mingled with the pleasure, giving me the ultimate high. I needed her to come again, now.

I wrapped my fingers around her neck and squeezed. She panted for air, air that I could so easily take from her, but wouldn't. Not today. With my other hand, I pinched her clit. That was all that was needed to push her over the edge. This time, she screamed when she came.

I thrust faster, following her over the precipice and into oblivion.

20

GEM

A huge, sweaty body caged me in on the couch. It smelled good, like honey with a hint of clove. That was the first thing I was aware of as I floated back to reality. My skin prickled with an overload of sensation—warmth, burning, aches. Every inch of me felt alive in the strangest way.

Flashes of images went through my head. Nathaniel taking me into a room, tearing off my dress, and spanking me. I licked my lips, tasting the metallic tang of blood.

Wait—*Nathaniel?*

I'd just fucked Nathaniel. No, not just fucked, I'd gone feral on him. I'd bitten him, but not marked him as my own. Yet.

Oh. My. God.

I peeked through my lashes at the man who was still trying to catch his breath. His blond hair was an absolute mess. His lush lips curved up in a smile—which meant this had to be a dream. Right? Nathaniel never smiled.

My gaze darted to his eyes. He was staring at me. Some of the ice had melted in those green orbs.

"Hey," he said.

Hey? How on earth was I supposed to respond to that? This was not a *hey* kind of situation. He'd spanked me and I'd liked it—a lot. His rough hands had left bruises all over my body, yet I didn't feel abused. He'd been brutal, but it only brought me pleasure.

I was so damn confused right now. Given my past experiences, none of what happened in here should have been okay.

Was it okay?

I'd drawn blood. His blood. Was he okay?

I shifted uncomfortably beneath him, only then realizing his dick was still buried deep in my pussy. It was so intimate. My cheeks flamed.

His brow furrowed. "You okay?"

"Um. Yeah, I'm fine."

A frost glazed over his eyes. "What did I say about lying?"

Shit.

"Uh... not to?" How lame of an answer was that? In my defense, this was awkward as fuck. I might be freaking out a little, and I was still trying to wrap my brain around what just happened.

"Tell me what's wrong?" He smoothed my hair away from my damp forehead. The gesture was so caring, and unnerving coming from him, that I simply gaped up at him, speechless.

Finally, I said, "This." I motioned between us. "This is wrong."

"What's wrong with this?" he drawled.

"Everything. You don't even like me."

"You don't like me either." His smile returned, crinkling the corners of his eyes.

"I never said that. I don't know you."

"Now you know me a whole lot better." His lips twisted into the cockiest grin ever. "Wouldn't you say?"

I sighed. "This was not supposed to happen."

"This was inevitable." He brushed a kiss at the corner of my mouth. "Can't you feel the mate call between us? I knew it the first moment I saw you."

"You did?" I scoffed. "And you've been cold and cruel all this time. Why?"

"Yes." He captured my wrists and pinned them above my head. "Because you neither want nor need a mate like me, Gem. I'm bad news. I'll ruin you. I didn't mark you, so there's still time for you to take Kevin and Blake and run. Run far away. Just know that I'll never stop hunting for you. They'll ruin you too, but not like I will."

Run away? Never.

"You don't scare me," I said softly.

He seemed baffled, a hint of his scowl returning. "Even after everything I just did to you? You're still not afraid?"

I took a moment to consider his words. He'd know if

I was lying or not. I could have pushed him away, or screamed, or darted out of this room, but I hadn't. He was inside of me at this moment, growing hard again.

I undulated my hips, feeling him slide inside my sore, cum-soaked pussy. Everything he'd done to me I'd wanted, craved. I'd begged him for more.

None of this made sense to me. I wanted him as much as I wanted Blake and Kevin. He was the missing piece of my puzzle. With each of them I had a different kind of relationship dynamic. I hadn't even realized I needed what Nathaniel offered until tonight.

With Blake, my relationship was playful. Kevin was commanding and intense but caring and kind. Nathaniel was something else entirely. He brought my damage to the surface and made me embrace it in a way I needed yet didn't understand.

"I'm not afraid of you," I said, moving my hips again.

He closed his eyes and groaned. "You're so fucking perfect."

I faked a gasp. "Was that a compliment? Coming from the ever-brooding Nathaniel?"

He thrust into me hard enough to conjure a real gasp from my lungs. "You be a good girl, and there's more where that came from, honey."

"Then ruin me again. *Please*."

"With pleasure—and some pain."

After numerous more orgasms, Nathaniel called the guys to check in on the situation. Worry crashed into me and I tore at my thumbnail. Was my sister safe? Were Kevin and Blake okay?

Nathaniel nipped at my bare shoulder. "Everything is okay. Arik fled, his trail went cold, and they're heading back here."

"What about my sister?"

"Kevin called in a few favors. We have eyes on her, so she'll be protected until this is over."

I was grateful for that. "Thank you."

Nathaniel shot me an unreadable look, and a strained silence grew heavy between us. I decided to tread lightly, and cautiously, through this new dynamic. I wasn't sure how this relationship would unfold.

A light tapping sounded on the door broke the silence, and Nathaniel let Blake and Kevin inside. The room shrunk further with their enormous bodies crowded around.

Kevin handed a bag of clothing to Nathaniel, while eyeing me carefully. A slight crease appeared between his eyes. He took in the remnants of shredded clothing all over the floor with a lifted brow.

Blake was less subtle. He strode up to me and turned me around, touching every red mark and bruise on my skin. "You're hurt."

"I'm not. Not like you think."

Despite my words, he glared at Nathaniel. "I'm going to rip you apart for this."

I shrugged out of his grip and stood between him

and Nathaniel. "No one is hurting anybody." I pressed my back against Nathaniel's chest and he rested his palms lightly on my shoulders.

"You're a sick fuck," Blake roared at him.

Nathaniel squeezed my shoulders. "I am. And apparently, you don't know our mate half as well as you think you do. You see these marks on her?" He skimmed one hand down my torso and I shivered at his touch. "These are love marks. She likes them and wears them proudly. Hell, she tore apart my fucking back."

I blushed at the reminder of my ferociousness.

Nathaniel turned around so everyone could see the partially healed claw marks that crisscrossed his back and shoulders. That must have *hurt*, yet he'd only seemed more turned on each time I dug my nails into him.

Blake and Kevin exchanged a contemplative look. I was always soft with them, giving and taking pleasure, making love. It was the direct opposite of the aggressive, brutal sex I'd had with Nathaniel. Even our second round hadn't been that much gentler. Yet, both ways felt right. They felt true to my nature.

Kevin finally broke the strained silence. "You did that to him?" he asked me.

I nodded. "I did, yes."

"Good." His lips briefly quirked with a smile. "Get dressed, the night's not over yet. We're here to have some fun."

I slipped on a pair of tight black pants and a low-necked shimmery top, then retrieved my heels. The outfit wasn't as elegant as the dress, but it worked just fine for the club.

We spent a couple more hours at the nightclub dancing and drinking and chatting. At one point, Nathaniel perched me on his lap, which surprised the fuck out of Blake and Kevin—and me. I could tell by their stunned expressions.

Granted, Nathaniel didn't seem like the type who usually went for public displays of affection. I wasn't exactly sure how he usually treated his women, but apparently this wasn't it.

I was a little bit jumpy through the rest of the evening. Every shadow seemed to secretly conceal a waiting Arik. The guys never let me out of their sight for a second, even though they insisted Arik and his cronies were long gone.

Whenever anxiety threatened to overtake me, I reminded myself that I was safe with my three bears, and my sister was out of harm's way, too. This wasn't over, but I also didn't want it to ruin the rest of our night.

Kevin's... associates were out there protecting my sister and tracking down Arik. Everything would be fine.

Around three in the morning, we made our way back to the hotel. The idea of sleeping in one bed with the three of them didn't seem nearly as distasteful as it had this afternoon. In fact, I was looking forward to it.

The next morning, reality came crashing back in. We sat around a small table enjoying breakfast when I recalled the rest of what had transpired last night.

"Arik…"

"Is gone for now," Kevin said. "But I have people who are keeping an eye out for him. When he resurfaces, we'll know."

"What are we going to do? He won't let me go. At some point, he'll come after me again."

"We're not letting you go," Blake growled.

Kevin brushed his thumb over the twin crescents on my neck. "You're ours."

"I agree with them." Nathaniel scowled, but I didn't take it personally this time.

"Then what, we hide, fight?" I asked. I knew Arik, and once he set his mind to something, he was like a dog with a juicy bone.

"We'll return to our cabin," Kevin said. "Our security there is now top notch. We have the rogue wolf pack to deal with, then we will hunt down Arik. He can't be a problem if he's dead."

I glanced at each of my men's serious faces. They really were dangerous. I had a feeling I'd yet to see the extent of their ruthless natures.

"I think Arik knows where we live. He mentioned something about hearing that I was with three woodsmen. What if he finds the cabin?"

"It won't matter. Besides our security system, I have a couple of guards physically on the ground there to watch the place. Even so, we need to get home." Kevin stood. "We'll go on a vacation once this is all over. Pack up, we're leaving."

The ride home was much more comfortable than the one out of town, except for Blake and Nathaniel's game of stealing me out of each other's laps. They were treating me like a doll they didn't want to share. I snarled at them, putting an end to that, then appeased them by sprawling across both their laps.

As we wound up the mountain road, my nose tickled with the scent of smoke. By the time we pulled up to the garage, the column of flames in the valley below was visible. There was only one thing that could be on fire down there—our cabin.

"What the fuck?" Blake snarled. "Where are the guards? Did you get a call?"

Kevin shook his head, then opened his door and stepped out. "Nathaniel, you're with me. We're going to go check it out. Blake, stay with Gem. Both of you stay in the truck."

Nathaniel jumped out, leaving me with Blake in the idling vehicle. My mind created all kinds of dreadful images of what they'd find in the valley. It could be a trap. They could be walking straight into danger.

"We should go help them." I reached for the door handle, but Blake pulled me back.

"No. When Kevin says to stay put, he knows what

he's talking about. I've learned that lesson the hard way a couple, few, times."

"But what if they're ambushed?"

"They're far from helpless. Trust them, okay?" He coiled his arm around my waist.

My nerves grew rawer as the minutes ticked by, but Blake was right. We needed to stay put and wait for them to return. I had to have faith in them.

A low rumbling sound caught my attention. Blake moved to look out the windows, trying to locate its source.

"What is it?" I asked.

"I don't know. The noise is echoing off the mountains and I can't pinpoint where it's coming from. But it sounds like a—"

The distinctive thunderous whoosh of helicopter blades solidified somewhere above us. We had no time to react before a piercing whistle ripped through the air followed by a deafening explosion.

For a long moment, my sight filled with a ball of fire. The blast hadn't hit us directly, but it was close enough that the truck slid off the road, tipped, and tumbled down the hillside. I shrieked, trying to hold on to something, anything, but what was up and what was down kept changing.

Abruptly, we stopped when the truck smashed into a wide tree trunk. The impact had me seeing stars. I could sense Blake beside me, but something was wrong. He wasn't moving.

Metal creaked and groan as someone tore the door from its hinges. A hand snaked inside the cab, groping for me. It didn't smell like either of my bears, so I bit down on it hard enough to draw blood. It recoiled, only to come back as a fist.

The blow hit me across the side of my face and my vision darkened at the edges. Then I was being hauled out of the truck. A cloyingly sweet-scented cloth was pressed against my mouth and nose. I gagged. With my first inhale, the world dimmed then vanished.

21

GEM

Consciousness slowly returned. The world seemed fractured into bits and pieces. Some of them made no sense to my drug-addled brain. I smelled wolves, lots of wolves. Arik's face floated in front of my vision. Men laughed. Cigar smoke wafted through the otherwise clean forest air.

"Welcome home," Arik said, blowing smoke in my face, before he retreated from view again.

I coughed and blinked multiple times. Reality settled in my stomach like a lead weight. My body ached all over like I'd been tossed around against unyielding metal.

The truck. Blake. Was he okay? Were Kevin and Nathaniel alive?

I sat up too quickly and my head spun for a moment before steadying. Where in the hell was I? Where had Arik taken me?

I was lying in the corner of what appeared to be a large tent. In the center was a crackling fire surrounded by several men who were drinking and smoking. Their laughter sent a wave of nausea through my gut.

Arik was among them. When he noticed I was sitting up, he smirked and waved.

"There she is. My girl. She survived our daring rescue."

Rescue?

"Welcome home, babe," he said. "I have some old friends I think you'll remember. Sven, you remember Gem, right?"

Sven. He was the Alpha of the outlaw pack, the one who was trying to take my bears' lands.

But the man who rose and strode toward me was so much more than a mysterious pack leader. *Sven.* How had I forgotten?

His six-and-a-half-foot frame loomed over me. The scar that cut down one side of his face was the same as the last time I'd seen him. His eyes brightened with the glow of his inner wolf. The tip of his cigar flared bright red as he drew on it, staring down at me with a cruel twist of his lips.

Arik's voice floated through my memory. *This is how you make her scream.*

One side of Sven's mouth lifted in a grin. "Do you still wear our brands, wolf-girl?" Lust flashed in his eyes. "Let Uncle Sven see that pretty stomach that we marked up. I'll tell you, I can still hear your screams after all these years. You were the best I ever had."

I cringed away from him. He most certainly was *not* my uncle.

"Boys," Sven called. "I think we should commemorate this reunion with a repeat. Let's see if she'll scream just as long and loud as she did the first time. Arik, hold her down for us, will you, comrade?"

"It would be my pleasure." Arik, and three others, rose from around the fire. Their gazes locked onto me like I was their next meal, and Arik approached with swaggering confidence.

As soon as he was within striking distance, I kicked, shoving my stiletto heel into his thigh. He howled in pain and stumbled backward.

Sven laughed. "Seems she has more fight than she did all those years ago. This is going to be even more fun than last time. I can taste it."

I crouched in the corner, a low growl emitting from my throat. It was true, I had grown stronger while living with my bears. I was no longer the hopeless, pathetic mess that my pack and Arik, had turned me into. I'd discovered that I was worthy of a blessed life. I had three mates who *loved* me for who I was and would never think to abuse me the way Arik had.

They'd restored me to the feisty, curious, and playful girl I'd been when I was young. They had also united me with my wolf in a way I never thought possible. For all of that, and more, I loved them with a passion that consumed my soul. I certainly wasn't going to die here. I had too much to live for, too bright of a future ahead.

"Fucking bitch!" Arik nursed his bleeding wound. Unfortunately, he'd heal over the course of the day.

"You're going to regret that, Gem. Apparently, I need to remind you how to behave. You're a good little slut, babe, now take off your clothes and open your legs."

I snarled at him.

He lunged forward, his hands outstretched, reaching for me. My nails sharpened into claws and I swiped at him, tearing into his flesh. He retreated again, to examine his bleeding hands and arms.

I wasn't going to be able to hold out much longer. They were too large to take down in a fight. My only option was to run.

Twisting around, I slashed through the tent fabric and crawled through the hole. Only I wasn't quick enough. Someone gripped my ankles. I screamed as they dragged me back inside. Rounding on them, I slashed across their face.

The blow to the back of my head dazed me enough that I slumped forward. Strong arms caught me in a vice grip.

The next hit came from Arik. I recognized his punches, the way he liked to leave bruises but not crack bones. He wanted it to hurt, but not cause permanent damage, or at least that was what he'd once told me.

Then there were more hands on me, pinning me down as others tore off my clothes. A rough palm splayed across my abdomen, tracing the cigar burn scars in a way that made my skin crawl. I bucked against them, but to no avail.

A searing pain blossomed right above my belly button. I hissed. The scent of burning flesh, that I knew was my own, made bile rise in my throat.

Sven's face cut into my vision. "You should have screamed. Give Uncle Sven what he wants or he'll keep going until he gets it."

I spat in his face.

Slowly, he wiped away the spittle. "Boys, make her hurt."

22

KEVIN

"*Fuck!*" I paced near the smoldering house fire, and the bodies of the dead guards, with the phone to my ear. Lucas had me on hold while he located the information that I needed. I was one hundred percent sure that Sven and his pack had set fire to our cabin. How he'd managed to not trip any alarms that would have shown up as alerts on my phone, and taken out the guards, was still a mystery.

What I didn't know was who had taken Gem. Arik had threatened to nab her from us, but had it been him or Sven who'd kidnapped her? Last time Sven had her, he'd attacked and tried to kill her. Why change his mind now, and instead of finishing the job right here, take her with him?

Unless Sven and Arik were somehow working together. I didn't fucking know. I needed answers. Now.

Not far away, Nathaniel tended to a livid Blake. He'd been bashed around hard enough in the truck to get knocked out. Even so, he blamed himself for Gem's kidnapping.

Hell, so did I. I never should have left them in the truck. We should have stuck together and then Gem would still be here. Our cabin was unsalvageable, the truck was totaled, but I didn't give a fuck. Our mate took top priority.

My stomach burned. We needed to find her before anything bad happened. Whether it was Arik or Sven who took her, neither would be kind.

"Are you still there?" Lucas spoke through the phone.

"Yes," I barked.

"We did some digging. I texted you a list of Arik's associates. One of them is Sven. They've worked together on and off for years."

My vision hazed with crimson. Those two fuckers were going to die. Tonight.

"We're going after them," I said. "They have to be at that encampment Nathaniel tracked them to a couple weeks ago."

"We'll meet you there."

I hung up and scrolled through the text. As far as I could tell, there were no other names of interest on the list.

I approached the guys. "Arik is working with Sven. Chances are good we know where they took her, and they don't know we already have their location. Let's get moving."

None of us bothered undressing before we shifted to our bear forms. Our clothing tore to pieces, and I shrugged the remaining scraps off before lurching into the woods.

Nathaniel took the lead since he knew specifically where we were headed. The earth trembled under our paws as we galloped across meadows, through streams, and over mountaintops.

Hours flew by as we pressed ourselves onward. My chest clenched every time I thought of Gem in those bastards' hands. I wasn't naïve enough to assume they wouldn't touch her. They would touch her, and I was going to make them pay dearly for every moment they had our mate. For every mark, bruise, and fucking word they uttered to her, they would pay.

Another part of me grappled with guilt. We'd promised to protect her, and we'd failed. Because of our inadequacies, she was suffering.

I swore to myself that when we got her back, this would never happen again. We would always take potential threats seriously. Even scum like Arik would be snuffed out if he so much as looked at Gem. Better to shoot first and ask questions later.

The sun dimmed as it set behind the mountains, and cast our shadows, long and distorted, before us. We were headed due east. Soon, we wouldn't have the benefit of the sun's guidance and we'd have to rely on the stars.

Twilight deepened into night. We crested a ridge and halted for the first time. There, in another valley over, multiple columns of campfire smoke reached for the bright moon.

These stupid fuckers didn't even try to hide their

camp. They thought they were so isolated in the wilderness that no one would find them.

Well, we did. We were here.

Now it was time to make them regret every decision in their lives that had led them to this moment.

23

GEM

It was near midnight, or maybe the early hours of the morning. All I knew was that it had been dark for a long while. Even so, sleep refused to claim my numb mind.

Arik's naked body curled around mine like we were lovers when that couldn't be further from the truth. My skin crawled with tiny, invisible ants. My stomach churned, but I'd thrown up all of its contents many hours ago. The dry heaving had passed. My tears had dried up too. I passed the time staring up at the tent's ceiling.

I would say that I'd endured worse than this and survived, but... I wasn't so sure anymore. How did a person put all the warped and damaged pieces back together and carry on? If I was broken before, now I was shattered.

A growl pierced the quiet night. I blinked at the

sound, but otherwise ignored it. It meant nothing to me.

In the distance, a disturbance thickened the air and grew louder. A growl was met with a snarl, a tremor shook the ground, a scream was cut short, and all the while, I lay unmoving.

Arik stirred. "What the fuck are they doing out there?" He gathered his clothes and stood, not bothering with me. His confidence that I wouldn't move an inch spoke volumes. He'd truly broken me this time. I was a shell of my former self, bent to his will and ready to be used as he saw fit.

When he exited the tent, the air seemed to grow lighter. I could finally draw in a full breath. The weight on my limbs eased and my fingers twitched.

The sounds of unrest—no, *fighting*—grew closer and closer. Had my bears found me? A tiny leaf of hope unfurled in my chest.

Whether it was them or not, I couldn't stay in this tent. Arik or Sven would take me and use me as a bargaining chip. Or just kill me because they could. Either way, I couldn't stay in here.

I rolled over and agony struck me like lightening. I gasped and fresh tears sprang to my eyes. Pushing away the pain, I crawled to the flap and pulled myself through.

Outside, the moon illuminated several wolves running toward the commotion. Flashes of light that looked like spell craft sparked in the distance. Since shifters didn't have magic, I had no idea what was going on, or who was attacking the camp. Friend or a different kind of enemy?

I headed in the opposite direction, away from all the people, to where the dark, quiet forest beckoned. Naked, I stumbled through the camp, trying to get away from everything happening around me.

My bare feet padded across the spongy ground. I'd just made it to the tree line when the hairs on the back of my neck stood on end. Whirling around, I grabbed on to a branch to steady myself, and sought out the source of my unease.

My gaze locked with Sven's. He strode toward me, eating up the distance with long strides. His features were contorted into a furious glower. This time he was going to kill me. I could see it in his eyes.

With the thud of my heart pounding in my ears, I tried to run, but my legs refused to cooperate. I made it ten staggering steps before my knees gave out and I went down fast and hard. Pine needles and dirt clung to my skin.

I turned onto my back, using my arms and feet to scurry as quickly as I could through the underbrush. My gaze latched onto Sven and I couldn't tear it away. He was moving too fast. He was almost on me. His eyes glowed yellow with his inner wolf right before his body busted from his clothing and emerged as a pale brown, snarling beast.

I wanted to shut my eyes, but I couldn't. The moment seemed surreal, like it wasn't really happening to me, and I was watching someone else's last few seconds of life.

Time slowed as his massive wolf bunched its muscles and leaped into the air. Saliva dripped from his gaping maw. His fur flattened in the breeze created by his momentum. Closer, closer, and closer he came.

I finally closed my eyes and turned my head to the side as his form was about to collide with my body. I drew in one last breath, held it, and waited for the inevitable.

A *whoosh* moved the air across my face. I heard the crunch of bone as two bodies slammed together, but I didn't feel it.

Peeking through my lashes, time seemed to return to normal, as I watched Sven's wolf wrestle with two bears—one black and one golden. The sounds they made were awful.

I scooted away from their fight. Beside me was a partially rotted, hollowed log. I rolled under it, using it as shelter. The fresh, woodsy smell of damp earth and ferns brought a sense of security to my chaotic world. My heavy head dropped to the plush earth, my eyes closed, and the last thing I remembered was the snarls of wolves and bears.

24
BLAKE

I tore two wolves from my back and another from my leg. Blood matted my dark fur, the wounds burned and throbbed, but I pushed on. My mate's scent was in the air and I was desperate to get to her.

Nathaniel body slammed a wolf who'd lunged at my back. In turn, I swiped a massive, clawed paw across the side of the beast who leaped at Nathaniel. Both mutts fell to the ground with whimpers. But they were like fucking cockroaches; not easy to kill.

The five wolves we were currently fighting off regrouped and attacked again. We stood back-to-back, defending ourselves and each other as best we could. One wolf snarled and leaped at my face. Before the fucker made it even a foot off the ground, a bolt of magic connected with its body and it exploded into a mess of gore.

Kevin's old bosses had decided to lend us a hand with this situation. They'd been waiting for us at the base of the ridge when we'd arrived. It hadn't taken long to form a plan of attack, especially since the plan was pretty straight forward—sneak in and attack, taking them by surprise. It was my favorite kind of plan.

With this many damn wolves, I was glad to have the help of an Alpha wolf, a vampire, Fae, and witch. Sven's pack was fucked. As soon as we brought magic to this shifter fight, it was basically over before it even started. We just had to do our best to not get ourselves killed before the end.

It didn't help that these fuckers were insane. They knew they couldn't win this battle, yet they kept fighting. They refused to surrender. They left us no choice but to kill every single last one of them, which suited me just fine.

My instincts heightened with alarm. I scanned the area and spotted Sven marching through the forest. He was determinately focused on something in front of him. I followed his line of sight and spotted a glint of golden-red hair.

Gem.

There she was, running away from him and falling to the ground. Fury dripped like lava through my veins. Wasting no time, I nudged Nathaniel, and we both took off at a gallop toward Sven, the wolves at our backs forgotten.

My blood curdled when he shifted to his wolf form and launched himself at our mate. I pushed my legs harder, faster. I leaped into the air. Our bodies made a horrific, yet satisfying, bone-crunching noise as we collided.

Nathaniel was right behind me. The two of us dove on Sven, clawing, tearing, and ripping into his flesh. He snarled and yelped. We roared our rage into the night. With our teeth clenched around Sven's limbs, we tore him to pieces.

Nathaniel and I shifted to our human forms. He went to find Gem, as I indulged my unbridled rage by punching Sven's corpse until it was beyond recognition. Blood and gore coated my hands, arms, chest, and face. When I finished, I wished I had the power to bring him back to life so I could kill him all over again.

But it was done. The lawless pack no longer had their Alpha. And soon, there would be no member of this pack left alive.

My attention refocused on Gem. She lay limp in Nathaniel's lap, and my chest painfully tightened at the sight. Were we too late?

I sprinted the short distance to them. Fresh cigar burns peppered her pale skin, deep slashes cut across her stomach, and her gorgeous face was bruised and swollen. Was that a boot imprint on her thigh?

My entire body shook with rage and anguish. What had they done to my little she-wolf?

Nathaniel stroked her hair. His livid, watery gaze met mine. "She's alive," he said. "But she needs help."

Kevin crashed through the forest with the Fae, Cade, close behind him. Both of them swooped in beside us. Kevin's gaze took in her injuries, while Cade's hands glowed with healing magic. The Fae rested his palms on our mate, and an unbidden growl rumbled in our chests. The gutsy Fae ignored us and continued with his work.

The seconds ticked by in my head. Slowly, her flesh knitted back together, leaving pale pink reminders of the wounds that had been there before. His powers were such that she would have no scars from this experience, though her old scars would remain.

The crunch of pine needles drew my attention over my shoulder. A dark-haired woman approached us. Emma. We'd had very brief introductions before we attacked.

Instinctively, I inhaled. She smelled of wolf but carried a wand. She was a hybrid. Kevin had told me about hybrids, but this was my first time meeting a creature like her.

She crouched down and swept an assessing gaze over Gem. "Cade can heal her external wounds, but the internal, emotional ones are going to take much longer to heal." She spoke as if she knew this from personal experience. "Once she's stable, we'll teleport out of here."

The night grew quiet once again as the fight came to an end. Occasionally, a low whimper pierced the air, but they were repeatedly cut short.

Cade worked on Gem for another ten minutes then gave us a curt nod. "Let's go."

Kevin picked up our mate and cradled her against his chest. Nathaniel's fingers continued to stroke her hair, and I rested my palm on her shoulder, just needing to feel the comforting warmth of her body, to know she was still here and with us.

We'd found her, and rescued her, but a part of me feared we were too late.

"I'll take you four first," Emma, the witch-wolf hybrid, said. She gripped my arm, spoke a spell, and then we were surrounded by purple smoke. My insides twisted for several seconds as the world disappeared around us.

When the smoke cleared, we stood in front of a mansion nestled in a different kind of forest. Here the trees towered so high, I could barely see the tops. I noticed the distinct scent of sea salt mixed with the wet, mossy smell of the forest. Humidity swam into my lungs.

There was only one place this could be, Penumbra Mansion. We were in the Pacific Northwest, where the mountains and forest met the ocean. This was head-quarters for Kevin's old bosses, the notorious criminal organization, Penumbra Syndicate.

My fingers tightened around Gem's shoulder. This might be a safe haven, but I certainly wasn't letting my mate out of my sight while we were here. I knew all too well what type of men got their hands dirty in the supernatural underworld.

Kevin and Nathaniel had both been in it much deeper than I ever had. But still, I didn't want any of that to touch my sweet girl. There was a reason we lived in the middle of fucking nowhere—to get away from all of *this*.

Now we were back in the thick of it.

25

GEM

Penumbra Mansion was huge and mind-bogglingly impressive with its high ceilings, marble floors, and sleek design. I'd never in all my life seen wealth of this magnitude. Every time I entered a new room, I had to stand there and take it all in. This was real wealth, old money, not the fleeting paydays that Arik had from time to time when he'd splurge on something useless.

The thought of Arik made my stomach churn. We'd been here for a week, and honestly, the mansion was a welcome distraction for my nightmare-riddled consciousness.

Kevin, Blake, and Nathaniel never let me out of their sight. Their touches were more tender than before, like they were afraid I might crumble to dust, which I didn't blame them for thinking. Some days were better than others, but on those worse days, I was afraid I'd disap-pear into the darkest recesses of my mind and never find my way out.

It didn't help that Arik had escaped.

All the other wolves had been killed during the attack, but Arik was nowhere to be found.

My skin itched with the awareness that he was still out there, living in the same world as me. I jumped at every shadow, screamed at any loud noise, and refused to leave the confines of these walls.

Kevin was called away earlier this morning, so I sat on the balcony of our room with Nathaniel and Blake. We spent a lot of time in companionable silence these days. I was often consumed by my thoughts and trying to manage my unpredictable emotions.

They tried to be strong for me, but I could see the hurt and guilt in their eyes. They blamed themselves for what had happened to me. I didn't want them to, but I couldn't find the words to tell them that. It felt like a chasm had opened up between us and the more time that passed, the further apart we drifted.

I had no clue what could bring us back together. Could anything fill this void, or fix our pain?

Kevin entered the room. "I have news." His warm gaze landed on me and he hesitated before speaking. "We've caught Arik."

For a moment, the universe seemed to stop spinning. I couldn't breathe. I swore my heart stopped beating, an eerie silence stretching in its place.

He continued, "They are holding him at a warehouse outside the city. He's all ours. One of us should stay with Gem, while we—"

The world jumpstarted again. "I'm coming with

you." My own words surprised me as much as they did my bears.

Kevin's face softened. "Sweetheart, you don't have to put yourself through—"

"I want to come with you. I want to see him. I need this." I made my way to the closet and quickly dressed in a simple outfit of jeans and a light sweater.

Nathaniel watched me from the doorway, his gaze assessing. "You understand what we're going to do to him, don't you?"

I nodded. "Torture him. Kill him." I spoke those words, but they didn't seem to hold any meaning. All I knew was that I desperately needed to face Arik one last time.

"Those are easy words to say, but..." He raked a hand through his tousled-blond hair. "The reality of it is different."

I pinned him with my gaze. "I know. I lived through that reality."

So had Emma, the lady of the house. She'd visited me a few times and her words were what kept me going most days. She'd been through hell. But that hell had led to her living happily ever after with her three fated mates—a vampire, a wolf, and a Fae. Her story gave me hope that one day my life could hold such happiness too.

Backing down from a difficult situation was not an option. She told me the only way forward is through the anguish. On the other side was where she found her bliss, and the new version of herself, since the old one had died and been stripped away from her. I felt as though I was on the same verge. Facing Arik one last time was something I needed to do.

Nathaniel didn't say anything, but I saw the guilt shine in his green eyes. What I wouldn't do to erase it. But first, I needed to walk through the fire and emerge, if not purified, then at least freed.

"I'm ready." I stepped out of the closet. "Let's go."

We all turned toward the door and strode along the hallway. I was surprised Blake wasn't arguing with me. I shot him a furtive look and frowned at the deep scowl on his face. I looped my arm around his as we walked. He entwined his fingers with mine.

As we approached the front entry, I slowed. I hadn't been out of this house in all the time we'd been here. Taking this step felt monumental.

"You don't have to do this," Blake said, misinterpreting my actions.

"I need to." Releasing his arm, I stepped over the threshold. Outside, birds chirped in the spring drizzle. The sun momentarily peeked through the cloud cover. The world seemed so normal. I'd gotten plenty of fresh air out on the balcony, but being down here, on the ground, felt different.

A blacked-out SUV waited for us in the driveway. We piled inside. I spent the ride sandwiched between Blake and Nathaniel in the back seat, while Kevin followed the GPS's directions.

Forty minutes later, we arrived at a bland, weathered, blue warehouse that blended in with all the other blue warehouses surrounding it. The sky had darkened and steady rain pelted us when we stepped out. In the distance, I heard the constant thrum of freeway traffic.

A guard stood by the warehouse door. He greeted us with a nod, then allowed us entrance.

My gaze immediately found Arik. He was chained up and suspended so that only his toes touched the concrete floor. Around his neck was a thick metal collar. One side of his face was swollen, he was naked, and other than his face, he seemed unharmed. Beside him stood a table laden with knives and a variety of common tools—a hammer, several pliers, a blowtorch. On closer inspection, clear plastic sheeting covered the area under and around him.

The strange calm that had come over me since I learned of his capture suddenly shattered. A strangled sob tore from my throat. I was raw and hurting, beyond angry.

This evil fucker had used and abused me for his own gain. He'd manipulated me into believing that it was what I deserved. I'd just turned sixteen when he found me. *Sixteen*, barely more than a child, rejected by my family, and living in filth.

For nearly ten years he made me do unspeakable things and *thank him* for it, because it was the price I had to pay for food, shelter, and fleeting, fake affection.

The past couple of months with my bears had shown me what real men, good men, were like. They showed me true love and affection. They cared about me, beyond my basic wants and needs, to a level that was soul deep. From what I knew, they'd had hard lives.

They were deeply fucked up in some ways, yet they never treated me as poorly as Arik did on his best days.

And just like that, I was no longer under his spell. I was free.

Nathaniel nestled me against his chest, the embrace strikingly tender. "Do you want to leave? It's okay if you do."

I sniffled and shook my head.

"I'm going to do terrible things to him," he warned, his tone disconcertingly soft.

I wiped my tears away and gazed up at him. "I know. I want to watch."

He let out a wary sigh, then spun me around to face the scene before us. Kevin approached Arik, fisted his hair, and slammed his fist into Arik's face so forcefully that blood, spit, and teeth sprayed across the floor.

Blake took his turn next. He punched Arik in the side until his ribs cracked. Arik let out a pained groan.

"What's the collar for?" I asked Nathaniel.

"It's so he can't shift." His arms tightened around me. "It also makes it so he can't heal. He's completely vulnerable."

Oh. Interesting. I didn't realize such a magical device existed. Kevin really did have some very dangerous friends.

Once Kevin and Blake had their fill of pummeling that piece of shit, Nathaniel sat me on a stool and took his turn. Instead of punching Arik, he scooped up a knife and swiftly cut off Arik's dick.

Arik howled and fought against the restraints. Blood gushed between his thighs. Nathaniel fired up the blowtorch and cauterized the wound before he could bleed out.

A strange kind of tingling warmth spread through my chest and awakened my wolf. She took one sniff of the air, growled, then calmly settled in to watch the show. She especially hated Arik for turning me against her when I was younger. He'd told me she was worthless, useless, and I'd believed him.

Blake stroked my back. Kevin moved in close at my other side and rested his hand on my leg. We didn't speak. We just watched Nathaniel work.

He was skilled with a blade. Watching him was unlike anything I'd seen before. He took off long slices of skin while Arik begged and cried for mercy. He made promises, then threats, then more promises. All the while, Nathaniel's facial expression was set in an unreadable mask that never changed, never once flickered with emotion.

In that moment, I took to heart what Nathaniel had told me about himself. Everything Blake and Kevin had said about him finally made sense, too. He was a torturer. So skilled, he made it look like an art, and so experienced, that nothing phased him.

I should have been terrified of him, but seeing him like this made me feel safe, protected. Surely that wasn't a normal reaction, but that's how I felt.

My ears grew so used to the screaming that it practically became background noise. Or the soundtrack to a gory, bloody, surreal film that went on and on.

At one point, my wolf nipped and whined, restless. I

knew exactly what she wanted. I wanted the same thing.

Disentangling myself from my mates, I slid off the stool and approached Nathaniel. He curiously eyed me, some of the ice momentarily melting in his gaze.

I held out my hand. "Give me the knife."

26

NATHANIEL

I hesitated, unsure of her intentions. Was this too much, and she wanted to end his life quickly? Give him a mercy killing by cutting his throat and letting him bleed out? Then I realized that it didn't matter. All of this was for her as much as it was for us, so she could end this however she wanted.

I flipped the knife so I was holding the blade and offered her the hilt. "He's all yours."

She turned to him, a thoughtful expression on her gorgeous face. The knife I'd given her was small but sharp.

Tentatively, she dug the point in at the outside of his thigh. A trickle of blood spilled down his leg. Then she slowly sliced a shallow cut horizontally across his flesh. He twitched, but that was the only sign he showed that he felt her cut.

The bastard had stamina. We'd been at this for a couple of hours, and so far he had yet to lose consciousness, which I actually preferred. It was so much more fun when they were alert and participated in their own torture.

"Gem, babe, don't do this," he said. "Tell them to let me go."

I slammed my fist into his face. "Don't fucking speak to her!"

He swallowed thickly but shut the fuck up.

She continued to cut on him several more horizontal lines across his thighs that matched the ones I'd seen on her own legs. Had this fucker been the one who'd given her those scars? He cut on her?

As she continued, he hissed through the pain. Her cuts were superficial compared to some of the things I'd given to him already.

When she moved on to slicing across his stomach, he jerked on his chains.

"Don't," he said.

She ignored him and gave him the same number of slashes that were on her torso when we found her that dreadful night.

His face turned purple with rage. "Stop it, you fucking slut! You tell them to free me, or I'm going to fuck you 'till you bleed. You hear me, you worthless little whore? I'll—"

I silenced him with a fist to his stomach that was designed to knock the air from his lungs. He gasped like a fish.

Gem glanced up at me, her expression stony. "I want to cut out his tongue."

For a second, I was rendered speechless, then liquid warmth spread throughout my chest. "You do?"

"Yes. Will you show me how?" Her tone was calm and quiet, but I read the determination in her eyes.

My cock stirred. Could I teach her how to cut out a tongue? Hell yeah, I could. I reached for the pliers.

When I turned back to Gem, she said, "And then I want to cut off his balls."

Fuck. Now I had a raging hard-on. A vindictive Gem was the hottest thing I'd ever seen.

My lips spread with a slow smile. "I'd be happy to—"

"No!" Blake and Arik said at the same time.

I ignored the worthless fuck and turned toward Blake. "What's the problem?"

He glared at me. "You're not fucking corrupting her with your sadistic shit."

I glanced down at Gem. Did he even know our little mate?

She spoke first. "Blake, I need to do this. It's payback."

"Princess, please, I don't want you to do anything you're going to regret. Will you be able to live with yourself after mutilating him?" The pleading was clear in Blake's eyes.

I guess when he put it that way... Reluctantly, I said, "Gem, maybe—"

"Stop fucking babying me!" She waved the knife around. "He's not some innocent guy I picked up off the street to torture for kicks. He ruined my life, ruined *me*. If I don't get this rage out now, it will fester until it's all that's left of me. It will eat me alive. I have years of pain to take out on him. Help me. Please."

Be still my heart. I was more than ready to jump in and be her knight in bloody armor.

Blake opened his mouth, probably to protest further, when Kevin cut him off.

"She's made her decision," he said. "It would be wise of us to support her and see this through to the end."

After a moment, Blake gave a curt nod and let us continue.

Together, Gem and I did everything she initially wanted to and more. For hours, I showed her how to make him suffer, how to cause the greatest amount of pain, while making sure he didn't succumb to his wounds. Cutting out his tongue had been a brilliant idea. Never again would he call her names, and never again would *her name* fall from his lips.

She was a vision. If I hadn't fallen head over heels in love with her before that moment, this was it. My heart beat only for her. She was absolutely fucking perfect. How she could be covered in blood, yet still a shining beacon of light in my darkness, I'd never understand. But I didn't need to know all the secrets of the universe. I just needed *her*.

In the end, it was by her hand that he died. Together we watched the life leave his eyes, and his body go limp.

"Shotgun," Blake called when we approached the SUV.

I hid my smirk. He could have the front passenger seat all he wanted. I had plans for Gem in the backseat. Opening the door for her, she scooted inside and I followed. Kevin started the vehicle, and we made our return trip to Penumbra Mansion.

My cock ached and my teeth had already elongated and sharpened with the need to claim my mate, to mark her as my own. Beside me, she panted, and I could tell she also felt the mating call. I tangled my fingers in her hair and pulled her in for a kiss.

All the restraint we had left, snapped. She slid her hands under my shirt, while I undressed her as quickly as possible. Naked, Gem climbed onto my lap and impaled herself on my dick. We groaned in unison.

Blake turned in his seat. "The fuck? Now who can't keep it in their fucking pants?"

Gem and I ignored him. She rode me with punishing force, both of us chasing a climax that couldn't get there soon enough.

I knew exactly where I wanted to mark her. I'd had a bit of time to think about my options, so when the time came, I sank my teeth into the skin beside her left breast, right over her heart.

The taste of copper coated my tongue, and I lapped at the small wound that would leave a twin crescent-shaped scar. A moment later, her pussy tightened and pulsed around my cock.

"*Shit*," I murmured, coming deep inside her.

Only then did she take my hand in hers and bite

down on the fleshy part below my thumb. I grunted, reveling in the pinch of pain.

She collapsed against my chest and I wrapped her in my embrace. A genuine smile tugged at my lips. She was mine. I was hers. And as much as I'd hated the idea of taking a mate in the beginning, I couldn't have been happier in that moment.

"Hey," I whispered.

I could feel her smile against my skin. "Hey."

A raw tenderness that I'd never felt before opened in my chest. Words bubbled up in my throat and I knew I needed to say them, now, in this moment.

I tilted up Gem's chin until her blue gaze found mine. I mouthed the three most truthful words I'd ever spoken in my life. *I love you.*

Her smile was a burst of sunlight in my dark soul. When she whispered, "I love you, too," my stomach flip-flopped. I'd never thought I'd hear someone say that phrase to me and mean it. I never thought I deserved it.

But with Gem everything was different. I held her tight against me and sighed with contentment.

Blake repeatedly glanced at us in the rearview mirror, and Kevin wore a grin. My chosen brothers and I were bound by a bond stronger than anything we'd had before. Now we truly were family. All of us tied together forever by our she-wolf.

27

GEM

Back at the mansion, we went straight to our bathroom's en suite. Kevin turned on the double-headed shower, while we all peeled off our soiled clothes. There was no saving those, so they went straight into the trash.

Blake picked me up, my legs automatically wrapping around his hips as he carried me into the shower. He hugged me like he was afraid I was going to slip away. The water poured over our heads, and I nuzzled his neck.

"I'm okay, I promise. I'm still me," I told him. Cupping his jaw in my hands, I pressed my lips to his. "I'm sorry you had to see that side of me, but it's a part of who I am. It's a part I needed to let out."

He sighed. "I just don't want Nathaniel to twist you into someone you're not."

"He won't. I'm already twisted." With a faint smile, I smoothed my palms down his thick neck to his broad shoulders. "I was already broken and fucked up before I met any of you. Fate just saw to it that in you, I found my other half. You're perfect for me in every way. So is Nathaniel, just... in a different way. Same goes for Kevin. You're all unique pieces to my crooked puzzle."

Blake gripped the back of my neck and kissed me. His hot tongue tangled with mine and I moaned into his mouth.

Pulling back, he said, "I trust you. I believe you. And I'll wholeheartedly accept all parts of you, princess. The good, the bad, and the bloody."

"Good." I nipped at his full lower lip. "Then stop treating me like a breakable doll and fuck me."

"Are you sure that's what you want?"

"Yes."

He stepped forward until my back was pressed to the tile wall, then thrust into me with enough force to cause all the air to leave my lungs with a *whoosh*.

"Is this what you want?" he asked, setting a driving pace.

"Yes. Fates, yes."

"Do you want more?"

I eyed him through my lashes. "What do you mean?"

Behind him, Kevin and Nathaniel stepped into the shower. Their heated gazes were locked on me. I licked my lips and considered all the possibilities. Finally, I nodded.

"Hold on tight," Blake said.

I did as he commanded, as he spun around so that

his back was to the wall instead of mine. Then he dropped to his knees.

Behind me, Nathaniel crouched down on the tile floor. He pushed two fingers into my pussy, right alongside Blake's dick, and pumped slowly in and out. Using my own wetness, he stroked my other hole, giving me an idea of what he had in mind.

I moaned and dropped my forehead to Blake's shoulder.

"That feel good?" Nathaniel asked.

"Mmhm." I was at a loss for words. I turned my head to find Kevin standing beside me with his cock in his hand. He watched us with a hooded gaze and parted lips.

"Let's see how good you can take us all, honey." Nathaniel replaced his fingers with his thick cock. Inch my inch, he worked himself inside my ass. Blake stilled, allowing me to adjust to all the new sensations. I'd never felt so stretched and full. Every nerve ending hummed with pleasure, and just enough pain to heighten it to ecstasy.

"Good girl," Nathaniel said once he was fully seated in me. He and Blake set a slow rhythm that drove me wild.

I reached out for Kevin, wanting and needing him too. My fingers curled around his cock and I pulled him to my lips. He wrapped my wet hair around his fist as I opened my mouth and swallowed his length. Moaning, I closed my eyes.

"Eyes on me, sweetheart." Kevin's voice was rough, strained.

My gaze met his, using him as an anchor in this sea of pleasure.

Blake and Nathaniel picked up their pace. Kevin pumped his hips, his cock hitting the back of my throat and making my eyes water. His free hand cupped my jaw and throat. Other hands toyed with my nipples, and another found my clit. It was sensory overload at its finest.

Heat coiled low in my belly, the pressure building and building until it exploded, shaking my entire body. I screamed around Kevin's cock, and he erupted in my mouth. Nathaniel and Blake both cursed, then came inside me at the same time.

Before I could catch my breath, Kevin fell to his knees and kissed me with enough passion to make my toes curl.

We recovered by washing each other from head to toe, which resulted in two more rounds of group sex. By the end of it, I was afraid I had no bones left in my body and I'd never walk right again.

It was bliss.

We drove along the familiar gravel road. It had been a couple of months since the cabin burned down. Since then, we'd been staying at the mansion, but now it was time to go home. I had no idea what we were returning to since the cabin was gone.

Kevin handed a length of fabric over the seat to Nathaniel. "Blindfold her," he ordered.

My lips parted in question.

"It'll be my pleasure." Nathaniel wrapped the fabric around my eyes and tied it behind my head. "No peeking."

"You guys, what's going on?"

"Patience, princess."

I rolled my eyes at Blake, not that he could see me.

"Did you just roll your eyes at me?" His voice sounded nearer and I startled.

A blush crept over my cheeks. "N-no!" How could he tell? I was freaking blindfolded!

"Liar," Nathaniel said. "You know what the punishment is for being disrespectful."

I squealed when they made a grab for me. From scent alone, I could tell that Blake had dragged me into his lap, which meant...

Nathaniel lifted my skirt and his palm cracked down on my butt cheek. One... two... three times he spanked my ass. Being unable to see just added to the thrill of it.

"Fuck," Blake said. "You're so aroused. I want to taste—"

"We're here," Kevin barked, and the SUV halted.

Blake scooped me up in his arms and swept me out of the vehicle, then set me on my feet. Kevin took my hands in his. I could tell it was him by the callouses. His palms were the roughest.

He towed me forward. The crunch of twigs told me Blake and Nathaniel were close behind us. I let my other senses wander. The forest smelled the same as before, even with a hint of woodsmoke. Where was that coming from? Had they built a new cabin?

Kevin stopped. "This is for you." He slipped the blindfold from my eyes.

My breath caught in my throat. In front of me stood a cabin, but it was much larger than the one before. Blake opened the front door that was wood inlaid with glass, and I eagerly followed him inside.

A huge fireplace was flanked by floor-to-ceiling windows at the far wall. In fact, there were so many windows that reached all the way up to the vaulted ceiling, that I could see the forest all around us. Plush rugs, sofas, and chairs made for a comfortable sitting area.

A large dining table with an ornate chandelier was situated near the center of the open floor plan. On the opposite wall stood a gleaming kitchen with an enormous island.

It was both rustic and elegant at the same time. This cabin held every modern convenience, creating the ultimate luxury lifestyle within nature.

Leading to the second story was a curved staircase. I rushed up the steps to see what else had changed. Upstairs there were a couple of smaller bedrooms, and one huge suite similar to the one we'd stayed in at the mansion. It even included two walk-in closets and an enormous en suite. The bed was specially made to comfortably fit four.

The whole place was furnished, decorated, and ready for us to move right in.

Happy tears stung my eyes. Never in my wildest dreams had I ever thought I'd be this blessed. This cabin was my dream home, and I got to share it with my three loving bears.

Kevin brushed my tears away with his thumb. "Do you like it?"

I beamed up at him. "Like it? I *love* it. This is amazing."

Moving to the expansive windows, I gazed out at our tranquil surroundings. The outbuildings had been rebuilt as well in larger, better versions of what they'd been before. And was that…? I cocked my head to one side.

My mates came to stand at the window too. I turned to them. "Is that a helicopter?"

"Yep." Blake chuckled. "We thought it would help ease the sense of isolation. Getting into the city will be much quicker by air."

Holy shit.

"I don't understand how this is possible. Are you guys rich?" I gazed back out at the helicopter.

Nathaniel's smirked reflected in the glass, and he pointed at Kevin. "He's loaded. You saw Penumbra Mansion. They pay their people well. Though Blake and I aren't exactly paupers either. We wanted to give you everything. I hope we succeeded."

Tears threatened again. "I would have been happy living in a tent with you three. You know that, right?" I turned to face them.

Kevin looped his arms around my waist. "Of course, sweetheart. You make us so happy just as you are. And, hopefully, this will be more comfortable than a tent. Besides, I'm retired from Penumbra, but one never really leaves that life. So let's make the best of it."

"Thank you." I tilted my head back to look up into his warm hazel eyes. "I love you."

He kissed my forehead. "I love you too."

I twisted around and relaxed my back into his chest. Blake and Nathaniel each took one of my hands, and for a few minutes, we simply stared at the valley shadowed by the surrounding mountains.

This was home. I'd finally found my place in this big world.

Home. Family. Love. It was all right here, with my three bears.

Are you ready for more from this world? Read Her Wicked Mates for a dark Beauty and her Beasts retelling.

I would love it if you'd leave a review. Reviews are like tips for authors and we appreciate them so much!

ABOUT THE AUTHOR

Cassia Briar writes reverse harem romances.

She lives in the often misty woods outside of Portland, Oregon with her loving husband and several cats. Cassia's an avid reader with a TBR list so long, she'd have to become immortal in order to get through it all. Slytherin. Lover of coffee, gargoyle and monster art, rainy days, and the Oregon Coast.

Visit her website: www.CassiaBriar.com

SUGGESTED READING ORDER

ACADEMY OBSCURA SERIES
Her Forbidden Fae
The Flame Within
The Fiery Shifter
The Searing Trials
The Scorched Summer

VENOMOUS TIDINGS

HER WICKED MATES SERIES
Captive Beauty
Beastly Desires
Brazen Hearts
Twisted Fates

THREE WICKED BEARS

DEMON GAMES